THE VOYAGE

of the

UNDERGOD

THE VOYAGE

of the

UnderGod

A COMEDY BY KIRBY SMITH

FOUR WINDS
— PRESS —

SAN FRANCISCO

THE VOYAGE OF THE UNDERGOD

Four Winds Press
San Francisco, CA

FourWindsPress.com

ISBN: 978-1-940423-02-9

10 9 8 7 6 5 4 3 2 1

Cover illustration and design by Tanya Johnston
Interior design by Tabitha Lahr
Distributed by Publishers Group West

"Satire is a lesson, parody is a game."
—Nabokov

"There never was a great man yet who spent all his life inland."
—Melville

"No. He has work to do."

"Don't we all," says Father, gentlest of sighs. "Don't we all."

"What's his name?" asks Luther.

"God," says Mother.

"Eisenhower," says her witty husband.

The surf thunders and crashes and thrashes against itself. A wavelet emerges victorious, running to them up along the sand, attaining its natural limit, receding with a bubbly hiss.

"What if Indians attack my fort?"

"He will smite them," Father responds.

"God doesn't like Indians," Mother adds. "Because they don't take baths."

"Dad?" says Luther, seeking confirmation.

"According to this article," says Father with raised voice as if to drown out little voices, "the French forces at Dienbienphu are surrounded. They'll have to surrender. Pity, they look so brave."

"Where is Dienbienphu?" asks Mother.

"Vietnam dear," says Father. "Vietnam."

Once more the paper rustles. Father gives out a sigh more mournful then gentle.

Mother gathers the things together.

"Come on you little shortstop," says Father as Mother hands over the cooler. "Come on you little short stuff."

Luther takes a last look at his creation, which has been brought about with the aid of his trusty red shovel and his refusal to acknowledge the terrible blue of the distant horizon. Father, encumbered with cooler and paper, strides off for the parking lot, demolishing a corner of the fort with his feet, ignorant of his crime.

Then they are gone, on that long journey back to the middle states. Across the expansive land, past singing caves and moaning caverns and canyons to die for. Little of interest remains at the now-deserted stretch of sand: mute rock, the burrowing and scuttling of tiny creatures, the aimless energy of the tides.

An elderly man appears in swim trunks, making vigorous movements with his arms. He has been advised to take in the sea air and is doing so with a vengeance, in deep inhalations and expansions of his chest. He believes he will thereby prolong his days in the brightness of the sun, come that much closer to the age-old goal of immortality.

As he walks along the water's edge, the foam laps at his thinning ankles and a gull squawks in protest, rising with an awkward flutter out over the sea.

* * * * * *

Mother likes to tell of a crisp Christmas morning, preparing to bake a ham. She'd gone in search of six-year old Luther and found him out back, shivering, crouched behind the rosemary bush in eye mask and cape, brandishing a ray gun with a grooved hand grip—a present from Santa. Refusing all entreaties, he insisted he remain at his post to protect the family from invaders.

"What invaders?" she kept asking. Eventually, the exasperated child demanded of her in return, "Whose side are you on?"

"Your father's!" she replied, putting an end to the episode.

Tres amusant: a small boy sees danger where none exists, or could. For whatever else one thinks of the middle states, it must be admitted they are the isolated core of an isolated country and if and when the foreign invaders do come they will surely remain on the coasts, near the green of the ocean, where the weather is more temperate and the restaurants are better.

Father is a pharmacist referred to, even by wife Lydia in public interactions, as the Doctor. There is an arm chair of royal-blue felt in a living room corner across from the built-in cabinets with the good china and this is the Doctor's base of action when not filling prescriptions. From here, with the occasional glass of sipping whiskey set on an end table beside him, the Doctor reads his newspapers and magazines. The rise in women's skirts, the latest novel from a well-known recluse, the need to break the will of the enemy. All receive careful consideration.

He reads of a monk in flames in the streets of Saigon; a lazy glance across the page falls on a cartoon tiger extolling the virtues of the Esso brand of gasoline. The Doctor is a rational man and so it falls to him to fit such juxtapositions into his rational world. That he is able to do so is a tribute to his discipline, his upbringing and his lack of any imaginable alternative.

Lydia was fond of saying when she first met the Doctor that he lived "like a Shaker," a remark that would summon a wry smile to the Doctor's thin lips since he knew what Lydia did not, that the Shakers, besides crafting spare, wooden furniture, were socialists.

Roland Orr is Luther's friend. Sometimes Rollo, sometimes Rolio or Rolland from Holland (if you're not Dutch, an errant uncle used to say, you're not much).

Roland carries with him an air of perpetual activity: working on some gum, adjustments to a sock, checking the time, smoothing out a shirt or uniform.

He is a runner and he runs at odd times and places, across fields as if being chased, in deserted school hallways on trips to the fountain for water, after the school bus when it has long since gone.

In the midst of a milling playground Roland organizes mass games of tag but it is tag stood on its head: instead of one chasing many, the many all try to tag Roland and if they persist they eventually catch him and let go with triumphant whoops. Then it's on to something else, leaving Roland collapsed on his back listening to his own labored breathing and gazing at the wondering sky.

Luther is not much for being chased. He is a leader. He organizes games, arranging teams so he and Roland—the two best athletes—are together on the winning side. Once Roland, in idealistic rebellion, inserts himself on the weaker team to make it more fair. Luther sees Roland's point, but wonders why a person would place some notion of fairness gotten from who knows where, above loyalty to a friend.

Sunday mornings the Dorsey family attends church—in rain or snow or windy fall when spotted leaves meet delicious death under each tromping footfall. The Dorseys arrive early, they are always early, and are seated near the front. The pastor stands before them, above them, praying, signaling, wiping the perspiration: mediating between a Creator and his creatures can bring a sweat to a man's face.

Up, down. Up, down.

In obedience to the pastor and the cream-colored cross hanging behind him, they mix their voices together. An epiphany is presented, the seminal text put forth in clarion tones. Then settling into their seats for the main event.

Downward, Luther's glance as the pastor clears his throat.

Inward, the direction of a boy's imagination in the face of the expanding sermon.

Upward, the soul's ascent to Heaven.

Onward, the march of you-know-who.

Afterward, the grownups socialize and it is remarked how well-behaved Luther seems. Luther wonders what other way he could have behaved.

In the seventh grade Roland makes a casual remark to a girl from a different school. It is relayed to her brothers—the Fantastic Four, as they style themselves. Word comes back that Roland is done for. And the brothers do in fact corner him emerging from a record store, taking his new albums and flinging them like frisbees in a preliminary display of their powers. The deal is about to go down when Luther appears, as if summoned, and makes it clear anyone wanting to harm Roland will have to go through him. The Fantastic Four go away muttering dire threats, but are never heard from again.

Luther and Roland in high school: on a bench in the heart of a new shopping mall.

Roland says, "You want to see how to look at girls without them knowing?" Luther nods. Roland's jaw goes slack, his eyes empty out. He continues talking in a monotone.

"Take your mind somewhere else. Think about algebra. That way your face displays no emotion. Keep all your senses open."

"Open to what?"

"The moment."

"Christ," says Luther. "OK. So?"

"Did Karen Kaminsky just walk by?"

"Yeah."

"What was she wearing?"

"I don't know, I was looking at you."

"Tie-dyed tee shirt, corduroy bell bottoms with a peace sign sewn on the right ass cheek. And white boots like those go-go dancers. Her fingernails were powder blue."

"Looked like she just got 'em done," Roland adds, showing off.

"Wow," says Luther softly. Then, "Wow!"

"That's pretty impressive," he adds.

"Being in the moment," says Roland.

They watch a man arrange baked goods in a display window, betting on which pastry he'll touch next. An all-string version of Norwegian Wood slices through the indoor air.

out with their slanted eyes, praying to whatever strange gods they possess that the white devils will fall into their trap.

The United States Selective Service has taken note that Luther is of a fighting age and he's been invited for an interview. Lydia and the Doctor have a talk about being sensible, about taking advantage of the opportunities life presents, about couples with only a single child and how precious the life of that child can be.

"Pass the potatoes."

"Please."

"Pass the potatoes, please."

"Luther, how's that ankle?"

"What ankle?"

"The one you hurt water skiing a few summers back."

"Fine."

"Finish chewing before you talk. We'd like you to get it checked."

"It doesn't bother me any more. I played football on it this year."

"We would just like you to get it checked, dear. As a precaution."

"We made an appointment with Roy Walker. For Monday at three."

"I thought he retired."

"Well, he's been a friend of ours for a long time. We trust him. He's agreed to look at you."

Luther shrugs. "Okay. Does anybody want that corn?"

Luther's father hands Luther an envelope.

"I saw Roy Walker the other day and he gave me these. Looks like you've got some permanent damage in that ankle. This is a letter from Roy. He's recommending the Army not take you."

Luther nods.

Lydia says loudly as if speaking to someone hard of hearing, "You have to take these with you to your interview with the draft board. This is important medical information they will want to have. So they can make the right decision."

Luther's in line for a burger with Roland, who's drawn a low number in the draft lottery. Luther tells about the X-ray and Dr. Walker's recommendation.

"No kidding," says Roland. "I never knew that ankle was that bad."

"Guess it's the potential," Luther offers. "You know, maybe in battle the guys in my platoon are counting on me and my ankle would give out. I could endanger their lives."

"No chance of that happening now," Roland agreed.

They sit across a formica table top from each other late on a Friday night, tearing into packets of plastic ketchup, waiting for their order.

Roland says, "My dad talks about World War II. They invaded these islands in the Pacific. Japs had dug caves and all these tunnels. My dad says it was like a New York subway."

"Never been there."

"Me neither. The rock was too thick to bomb 'em out so you had to use flame-throwers. You had to get real close with bazookas and flame-throwers. He said he saw men burn alive."

Luther, salting his meat, says, "My old man never talks about stuff like that. But he supports this war. He says we either fight 'em over there or we fight 'em over here. Hey, she didn't give me the right change."

That fall while some young men are in that faraway land doing awful, faraway things, Luther makes a decision to attend Ohio State University. For the most part his academic debut brings him misery. The plight of the Huguenots fails to move him, the mysteries of Pythagoras are just as well unsolved, the utility theory of the economists is, to Luther, useless.

However in Theater Arts 101, an elective signed up for on a whim, Luther discovers acting, discovers that in the glare of the footlights he feels quite natural, and he is intrigued by the idea that simply memorizing his lines and repeating them with conviction can move an audience, elicit their applause. An applause that is not just gratifying, but self-affirming.

He declares a major in Theater Arts. He is punctual in attendance at all rehearsals, and he knows his lines and hits his marks. He puts in whatever effort is required. All in return for that magical moment when the murmuring dies away and the maintenance man with the mermaid tattoo draws back the musty curtains. Then Luther blooms like an overheated house plant.

In *Linus*, he shows a knack for romantic comedy as the near-sighted librarian finding a love that was there in front of him all along. As Babar the Elephant in *If Animals Ruled the World*, he is a wise and ponderous king.

But it is suffering he finds most compelling, the bringing to life of the tortured soul. In a script reading of Ajax, Luther again grabs the lead as the mighty Greek warrior who was put into a state of madness by the goddess Athena. While not in his right mind, Ajax slaughters a herd of sheep, mistaking them for an enemy army. Then with his sanity restored, he realizes the savage folly he's been made to do, and he falls on his sword in shame and expiation.

Professor Wilma Weimar is directing the play in the austere style of the Greek original. Luther argues that the death of Ajax should feature blood. He says if Ajax fell on his sword there would have been blood, a lot of blood, that movies show blood, that any modern audience enjoys movies and is accustomed to seeing movies and accustomed to seeing blood in movies and has moreover a right to see the blood of a man who has fallen on a sword whether from shame or expiation or simple clumsiness.

Wilma Weimar informs Luther in Teutonic tones that the enactment of his suggestion would violate the spirit not just of Sophocles, but of all Greek tragedy. Luther persists. Weimar says she would sooner see Hamlet appear on Jeopardy than have a drop of blood during Ajax, even in a classroom reading.

The day of the performance, as Luther/Ajax gives out an anguished cry of "O Death, Death, come now and look upon me," Luther feels under his tunic for a mini-balloon of stage blood procured from the prop closet, and when he falls forward on his broom-handle sword red liquid spurts forth in a stream of artistic purpose, soaking the pants of a front row observer, collecting in pools on the chipped and graying tile floor.

Weimar stops the production post-haste, then herself hastens to the office of the Theater Arts Department dean. A lengthy hearing is convened at which Weimar argues Luther is no better than the thugs disrupting classes and destroying property in the name of "peace". Luther says he has nothing in common with such as these and has harmed no one except the unfortunate front row student. He offers full reimbursement for the student's pants, while noting they had a well-worn look.

The dean, in his ruling, commends Luther for his artistic authenticity and waives payment for the red-stained pants, but suspends Luther for three months from all performances of the Theater Arts Department.

The suspension could have afforded additional time to focus on academics, but serves instead to lessen Luther's productive activity in general. His room, normally untidy, takes on a hazardous aspect. He makes

"It isn't much to launch a career vith, is it, my little *hasenfus*?" she asks playfully, employing the German word for a man of faltering courage.

"Take this vith you." She tosses him a rabbit's foot obtained during one of her Central American excursions. "For goot luck."

The Doctor and Luther spend a Saturday afternoon wandering the auto row, emerging joint owners of a pre-owned, persimmon-colored Pontiac Le Mans boasting 389 cubic inches of get-up-and-go, nestled into the widest, longest passenger frame Detroit has ever made. The seats are white vinyl and the chromium instrument panel is canopied like a jet's.

The night before the departure, the Doctor goes over his recommended route with Luther. The first stop of note will be Mt. Vernon in downstate Illinois for a visit with the Doctor's brother Earl, with whom there has been only sporadic contact in recent years. Earl's name and exact circumstances are generally discussed in muted tones of concern.

Lydia says, "Tomorrow I'll make a big breakfast, sausage and pancakes and orange juice like you always like. Maybe some coffee cake too. I'll just run and get some."

But next morning Luther wakes with the song birds and slips downstairs to make peanut butter and jelly on toast. He is waiting by the door with his packed bags when Lydia comes down not understanding, followed by the Doctor, grave and sleepy. Luther explains he wants an early start, doesn't want to be any trouble. Nothing he says could have troubled her more. The Doctor, straining, insists on carrying the bags out to the Le Mans, where they say their muted good-byes.

Luther first heads west for the recommended sightseeing in Chicago. He finds a motel and stays up late watching TV, sleeping in the next morning, then putting away a breakfast of sausage and pancakes and foul-tasting orange juice.

The next morning he heads downstate, arm dangling out the window, taking in the alternation of eastern forest with western prairie, dredging up from childhood the memories of his only uncle: tall, drink in hand, loud and sure of himself, winning at horseshoes, razzing them all; Lydia looking on uncertainly, laughing at what she infers are joking remarks; Luther's father patient, uncharacteristically sheepish. Earl had a long face ending in a set jaw, and cavernous eyes holding secrets he thought everyone could see. Luther has been told he takes after Earl more than he does his own father.

His second day on the road, Luther arrives in Mt. Vernon. The street he wants turns out to be an out-of-the-way cul de sac; the arriving Luther sees three police cars parked at odd angles, blocking the driveway of an aging two-story with a peaked roof, furthest from the main road. The house's paint is peeling, the front lawn is smallish, surrounded in its entirety by an uncared-for fence, and both house and lawn are dominated by a wide-blooming magnolia.

Neighbors are gathered, but none too close. An officer holds a bullhorn. To confirm what he somehow already knows, Luther asks where Earl Dorsey lives; a boy points to the rundown house. Luther asks an officer what's going on.

"Hostage situation. Crazy Earl's got his insurance agent inside."

He gives Luther a suspicious look.

Luther explains, "I'm Earl Dorsey's nephew."

"I'd have guessed that. What brings you here?"

"A visit. Here for a visit."

The officer speaks to a fellow officer holding a bullhorn, whose badge proclaims him Chief. They eye Luther as they talk.

"You kin to Earl Dorsey?" the Chief calls over. "Think you can talk some sense into him?"

"Don't know him that well. I can try."

The Chief shrugs and pushes the bullhorn button. "Earl! You got family here. Your nephew! We're sending him in."

Luther asks, "Is he…armed or anything?"

"Oh, he says he is but you never know what to believe coming out of Earl's mouth. He's just a little off kilter today, is all. Go on. He won't hurt you."

Luther pushes through a creaking gate, climbing steps to a paper cup-strewn porch, dusty webbing in the corners. The cups look to have recently held some kind of greenish liquid. The front door opens before he can knock.

"Luther? Little Luther? That you? Don't stand on that porch all day. Get inside."

It's Uncle Earl all right. Luther is tall enough now to look him in the eyes, which are set in an assessing squint as they scan the scene over his nephew's shoulder. The uncle's hair has thinned but there's no grey and his manner is brusque and vigorous. He shakes Luther's hand and almost crushes it.

There are no lights on inside. Luther's eyes need time to adjust. A row of open windows in the back let in a breeze which toys with the delicate, white curtains, making them do a ghostly dance. Luther notices with alarm a hand gun on the floor in front of a couch and a twelve-gauge shotgun standing in a corner.

Luther says, "What's going on? They seem pretty serious out there."

"They're just soreheads."

"They say you've got somebody in here."

Earl winks. "They mean Gene Farber. I let him sneak out the back a while ago. Told him to go home and sit in the dark with the lights off until I gave him the word over the phone."

Earl laughs. "Bunch of geniuses out there. Thick as the frogs of Egypt. How many does it take? Hand me that ammo clip."

"Geez Uncle Earl, I don't know if I should."

"For crying out loud."

Earl retrieves the clip himself and loads the pistol.

"You're John's son all right. Can you at least make me a mint julep? There's ice in the cooler. Grab a drumstick from the fridge if you're hungry."

"Uncle Earl, what's this all about?"

Earl whirls and sticks the pistol out an open window and fires off a few rounds.

"Earl!" comes the megaphone voice. "Stop that foolishness! You'll hurt somebody!"

Earl snorts. "I'm aiming high. Might hit a bird is all."

He's on his haunches, facing up at his look-alike nephew. Luther sits on the stairs that lead to the second floor landing.

"How's Lydia?" says Earl. "Your dad still sink into that armchair every night with a Scotch and a magazine? I don't know how she puts up with it."

Luther says, "Well yeah, now that you mention it. Pretty much."

"He was always that way. When we were kids he drank colas and read the funnies. What are you doing here anyway?"

"On my way out to Hollywood. Be an actor. I want to become an actor."

"The moving pictures, huh? No kidding. It's great to be young."

"Earl!" says the megaphone. "We're not spending Saturday night baby-sitting you! Come on out with your hands over your head!"

Earl yells back out the window, "Down with the Kaiser! Down with the Federal Reserve! It's our money, not theirs!"

He fires off another round with the handgun, then loads shells into the twelve-gauge.

"That'll give them something to think about," says Earl. "This whole thing started with an insurance settlement that thieving Gene Farber was keeping from me. But it's bigger now. A whole lot bigger. You ever hear of the Essence From Within? No? What do they teach you in those schools?"

"County fair," he answers. "They got burgers, chili burgers, cheese-burgers, chili-cheese dogs, drinks, fries. There's no entry fee neither."

He lifts the hood.

"Ice cream swirls too," he says, peering around the raised hood. "Almost forgot those."

"Sounds good," says Luther. "Is there an Indian reservation around here?"

The attendant steps back in surprise, oil dripping from an un-wiped stick.

"Indians? No. They all got killed a long time ago."

He administers the final touches to the windshield with the squee-gee, a careful wipe to end each swipe.

Leaning in with the change, he says, "Down the road from the fair-ground entrance is a bar run by a fellow named Harlow. I do recall him once talking about some kind of preservation around about there. He was trying to drum up customers for it. You can't miss it. Just head for the big ferris wheel goin' round and round and round. Have a nice day."

A few miles out of town the ferris wheel appears in steady, joyful ro-tation. To avoid paying for parking Luther drives a bit further and pulls into a gravel lot in front of a squat, adobe building sporting a neon sign hung above the front door. It says Harlow's. Sticking his head inside, Luther sees only chairs upside down on tables and juke box lights blink-ing as if in remembrance.

The fair is disappointing: cotton candy, livestock displays, the lat-est in kitchen appliances. Luther is about to head out when he hears a friendly call.

"Beer here. Cold beer. Looks like a hot one tonight. How about you, young man?"

Many beers later Luther finds himself more engaged with his sur-roundings. He sits attentively during a demonstration of sheep shearing. He listens to a bleating goat said to be preaching the gospel. Behind the flaps of her darkened tent Madame Sarajevo, smoky-voiced and wrapped in turquoise veils, foretells his death by water. At the history exhibit of Professor Moriarty, he learns of the scorched earth of Sherman's march to the sea and the cracked earth that results from geologic fissures and the still earth that is always around us but rarely noted by historians. He encounters varmints, varlets, vendors of homemade jam, the pleadings of a one-legged man, a once-noble colonel with a case of the jim-jams. A display of fireworks that flares in the sky and discharges in a thousand pieces, falling harmlessly below, leaving all as it was before.

In a wobbly folding chair at the foot of a makeshift stage he plops down to hear the rhythm and feel the blues. The diminutive Gus Johnson and his band. Gus in candy-cane-pinstripe with polka-dot kerchief peeking out playfully from the breast pocket. Luther's mood is just right for the full-on horn section and the snare drum snap and dash. Interesting too, the low swinging voices and high swaying hips of the trio of backup singers. Most interesting: the long dark lashes and demure smile of backup singer number two. By the middle of the second set Luther is pretty sure she is—cautiously, mischievously, perhaps not even intentionally—responding to his admiring gaze.

Near the end of the final set, Gus Johnson announces in his speechifying manner that the next song will be sung by Esther Frazier, and backup singer number two slips forward into an unhurried rendition of the neglected old ballad, *"Strangers When We Met"*.

Luther's drunken heart goes spongy, his spongy brain goes soggy and his eyes, normally clear and sure, glaze over with longing. Her last note lingers like summer's final eve. As the band loads their gear into a waiting van Luther finds himself in a somewhat slurred conversation with Esther. She invites Luther along to the club where they like to unwind after a show. She watches to see how readily he accepts, then how readily he crowds into the back seat of Gus's red Lincoln.

At the club, though the patrons' skin colors are a wide variety of shading and tincture, only Luther's can fairly be described as white and she studies his reaction again as they walk in the front door together.

They drink beer and shoot pool and they all like Luther well enough. Close to the end of one game Gus says playfully, "Let me show y'all how to stick it to Whitey," but he misses a blue-striped ten looking swollen on the lip of a corner pocket and knocks the black eight in instead. Luther is a gracious winner.

Esther's never been to California. She talks of growing up in the projects in Chicago. She interrupts one of Luther's stories to say, "Why you lookin' at my hair like that? You never seen a black person's hair before?"

"Well, we don't—there weren't a lot of black persons at my school. At college there were more. But of course I've seen a black person's hair before."

"Maybe not this close up."

"Maybe not this close up."

She moves a little closer. "So let me ask, would you bring me home for dinner?"

"I'm a long way from home," Luther says. "But if there's a restaurant around here, I'd like to buy you something."

"What if we was right round the corner from your folks' place? And what if we had dated for, let's see, six months. Would you take me home to meet your parents?"

She moves even closer to flick an imaginary piece of lint off Luther's shoulder and looks him in the eyes. Luther's gaze flickers down and away, then back again hopefully as if it had never been gone.

"Yes I would."

Esther says, "Okay. I see how it is."

They all pile back into the Lincoln and drop Luther off at his car and Esther walks over with him, braceleted arm around his waist. Eluding his friendly advances, she returns in her deliberate way to the waiting

Lincoln and off they go with a few cheery honks, leaving Luther alone, bedazzled and looked down on by a starry sky.

Music is coming from inside Harlow's.

The song ends as he enters; all he can hear is the scraping of his shoes on the floor and mechanical sounds from the juke box loading another disc.

A bartender wipes glasses. A slouching customer nurses a drink in the corner beneath a mounted TV playing an old movie, a western about a wagon train. The sound is muted.

Bartender holds up a bottle and makes a quizzical face.

Luther says, "Why not?"

Bartender slides over a poured glass as Luther claims a stool. Bartender is leathery, worn and weary. He says, "That your car out there? What kind?"

"Pontiac."

A sharp moan from the slouching customer, as if in sudden pain.

The bartender leans closer and says "Do you know where that word comes from? What it means?"

"I don't know. Is it a lake?"

"No. Pontiac was an Indian chief."

"No kidding."

"Yes. He was a great leader."

"Well, what was so great about him?"

"You had to ask," the slouching man says, knocking back his drink.

Bartender fills all their glasses. He says, "Who do you think colonized this country?"

"Trick question?" says Luther, looking around. "We did. The Americans."

"Perhaps you mean the British," the bartender says helpfully.

"Well, yeah. That's what I meant."

"I'm talking about *this* country, *this* land. Where I'm standing. The land of the Mississippi River from New Orleans through Michigan and

* * * * *

Shunning the main roads Luther continued west, seeking out strangers and new experiences, following signs advertising the fiercest porcupine in captivity or enormous heads chiseled in rock of great and mighty leaders. At roadside stands he tasted produce, inquired for cheap accommodations and told people who he was and what he was doing. He realized dimly that the Doctor was right, this was an adventure he might never repeat and he fell in love with it: the flat, inscrutable land, mornings painted in vermillion sky, big-eared rabbits' mad dashes away from the path of his onrushing headlights.

He ate stew with a trucker complaining of back pain and an amphetamine habit. He had his cup topped off by a waitress urging him to stop in Bakersfield for a visit with a hard-luck sister. He licked a vanilla cone at an outdoor table next to a Dairy Belle surrounded by chatting parents whose children ran around like savages.

He experienced a kind of traveler's euphoria. He had a wad in his pocket (the Doctor's cash) and gas stations up ahead—an unlimited supply—and paved roads to take him where he chose to go.

Approaching the Rockies across Wyoming's high desert after a shower had left the sky an inescapable blue he crested a hill, seeing first the arc of a dissolving rainbow, then spreading before him on both sides a ribbon of river halving in two an aspen forest in lockstep yellow. Pheasants scooted into the brush. And it came back to Luther all at once, what he'd read somewhere: the aspens turn golden in clusters because their roots are connected. And Luther, immune thus far in his young life to the hippie mantra of one-world love, felt for the first time a transcendence, a genuine outward surge. If there had been a way then and there to embrace the world and all its occupants, or to shake the Invisible Hand in thanks for his present feeling of infinite freedom, he would have done so. Then the Pontiac ran out of gas.

Luther got out. The road was an empty line in both directions. The only sound the whistling wind. As it died away Luther could hear the aspens quiver and the lowing of distant cattle. Seconds before he'd starred in the role of continental conquistador. Now he was but a young man with uncertain prospects, on his own in a world made vast. Where the crowded streets, the comfort of their bump and bustle? How distant the horizon seemed. How tinny the fairground songs, echoing from far away. He thought of Lydia and the Doctor, of crystal balls and searching eyes. Of a kite let go from a string, rising to forever. Was he really alone? Where was God? All around? Or not around at all? Luther was kneeling. A handful of dark earth slipped from his fingers.

He was no philosopher—that was decided then and there. Practical problems required practical solutions. Ultimate reality was for the professors to figure out. He snatched an empty can from the trunk and stuck out a thumb. His future awaited; it was scrawled on a scrap of paper in the flap of his wallet.

He was picked up by a rancher on his way to Laramie for a class on how to be a rodeo clown and driven back from the gas station by a rodeo clown from Laramie who'd always wanted to work on a ranch.

He sped over the Rockies and beyond, stopping not for great salt lakes nor pine tree resorts nor even the little fluffy clouds hanging in the lucid skies over northern Arizona like signs from those who watch from above. Before Luther knew it he could see the lights of Hollywood.

II

HIS AGENT WAS FAST-TALKING, rumpled, a kind face sifting through papers, fingering a rolodex as he instructed the youth standing before him with hands stuffed in jeans, head crammed with dreams.

"Luther Dorsey. That's okay, that's pretty good for a leading man. I'd keep it. It's not Tyrone Power. That's the best leading man name ever. Unless you want to do characters but from the looks of that square jaw and that head of hair you ought to go for leading man. Besides, who drives out from Ohio to do characters? I can't loan you money, which you probably need so find a job, anything. Call me in two weeks if you haven't heard. Thanks for coming down."

Six weeks later the agent called:

"Good news. You have an audition. Thursday."

"Thank God. I've been working at a car wash."

"Sure, you gotta pay the bills. This is a commercial. White Sail after-shave."

"Do I have any lines?"

"Most likely you smile at the camera and some bimbo strokes your face. If they like the spot you'll be seen all over the country. Great exposure. Plus you get the residuals."

"Anything I should do to prepare?"

"No. Well, don't enter any prizefights."

"You know, I use White Sail! Should I mention that?"

"Listen kid. Show up on time, stand where they tell you to stand and smile when they tell you to smile. My girl will call with the details. Let me know how it goes."

The ad was a two-parter, the first a bathroom setting in which Luther applied the product, eyeing his reflection in fulfillment. The second, climactic scene took place on a small sailboat with San Clemente Island as a backdrop. Luther more or less fondled the wheel in a white turtleneck and sailor's cap with gold trim, surveying the distant horizon as a redhead eyed him seductively. The only direction Luther received was to look "navigational."

The shot worked well, though no one could put a finger on why. Pleased execs at White Sail approved it for nationwide saturation.

After-shave sales at the time were vigorous, part of a backlash against the unkemptness of the '60's. But something in this ad struck a particular chord in the psyche of the American male. White Sail sales soared and the ad ran unaltered for nearly a decade, racking up consistently high grades in focus groups and surveys, and at the cash register.

There was even a famous parody with Chevy Chase as Luther, distracted by his own reflection, crashing against an oil tanker, causing a massive spill. Competitors tried to replicate the ad's success using sports cars, skydives, even a spoof with an astronaut in a zero-gravity environment. But nothing beats the sea.

To those in the biz the campaign was legend, although the reasons why remained obscure. In conversation with the well-shorn editors of

Bristle: the Journal of After-Shave Advertising, a White Sail bigwig gave his somewhat post-modern assessment: "It isn't that Luther Dorsey looks like he should be sailing into the wind with a beautiful woman eyeing his broad back suggestively. The spot works because Luther Dorsey looks like he should be *in a commercial* sailing into the wind with a beautiful woman eyeing his broad back with longing, or some such emotion."

Luther bought a home in the pleasant suburb of Santa Domingo. A financial adviser steered him to several lucrative shopping-center investments. He soon had income from rental properties and steady commercial work to add to the ongoing payments from the good people at White Sail.

Luther became a man of leisure. He could be found most mornings, long after the neighbors had left for work, padding down a sun-splashed walkway to take in the newspaper in what he hoped was an unobtrusive robe, or out to the mail box in the afternoon in pressed slacks and polo shirt to see if a residual check had arrived.

As with all success, Luther's was a mixed blessing. His agent would call about a role in a film and the response was invariably, "Sorry, this isn't a sailing picture." Luther was typecast. Nevertheless he was tall, dark, single, and he knew how to engage a person in conversation and make them feel important. There were women, sports cars, drives along the coast on the way in from a night of debauchery or the way out for a day of debauchery—top down, sharing champagne, women's hair streaming in the wind in shades of honeysuckle-blonde and dark cherry sable (his agent was active with several shampoo accounts).

There was also the luxury of time in which to think and reflect, breakfasting with the business section or munching a favorite crab sandwich with the kitchen radio on. He formed opinions on issues of public concern. He felt his own success as proof of how good the country was and what it had to offer, and found himself resenting those who tried to tear it down.

Luther eventually landed some non-commercial parts, the first coming in Scorcese's earliest Hollywood offering, the underrated *Choir Boys*, with Luther playing the tone-deaf Rocco. This led to appearances on behalf of local schools to promote music education. Luther found he enjoyed giving back, interacting with local leaders.

He landed a part in the long-running NBC western, *The Straw Men*, portraying the argumentative Sheriff Gibbs for two years until a fall from a horse during rehearsal robbed him of his rolling gait. The scriptwriters had him shot in the back by a Boston schoolmarm, and Luther settled with the show's insurers for a lucrative sum.

One more memorable role was Kit, the President's drunken, under-achieving first-born in the PBS miniseries "Fathers and Sons: Anything You Can Do, I Can Do Better." Luther left the production following a high-profile disagreement over the reasons for his character's troubling behavior.

Always with time on his hands, Luther liked driving into the Santa Domingo foothills to visit close friend Saul Blomberg. Saul was the deeply religious founder and president of the Precepts Corporation, an enterprise Saul described as concerned with "public relations in the broadest sense of the term." If pressed for specifics, Saul would launch into a bit of shtick, hunching his shoulders and extending his arms, palms facing up in apology and say, "If you have to ask, we can't help you." Precepts got results and left no fingerprints. That was all anyone needed to know.

There were outings on Saul's little "dinghy" (others called it a yacht) where Luther made the acquaintance of other responsible and productive individuals. There were jocular foursomes with high-rolling competition on the putting green and good-natured ribbing on the 19th hole;

horseback trots along old fire roads, excursions to out-of-state game ranches stocked with the elusive wing-clipped quail. Luther was impressed with Saul's crowd: their accomplishments, their knowledge of the way the world worked and how they made it work for them. They in turn took note of the personable young man who knew how to listen when talk got serious. A consensus formed within this select circle that Luther Dorsey was a comer: bright, articulate, blessed with a rare gift for connecting with people.

Over drinks around Saul's kidney-shaped swimming pool, he and Saul would hold forth on the problems of the day: a liberal bias in the media, troubles brewing in Central America, a weakened military, the drift to Darwin.

Luther ran into Esther Frazier at a club and would sometimes bring her to a social gathering hosted by Saul or an illustrious friend. Esther was treated with politeness and deference, even asked to sing a song or two, but a consensus eventually formed: with her hoop ear rings and unrepentant afro and too down-home ways (bringing her own potato salad to catered events), she wasn't a good fit for Luther or the lifestyle to which he so clearly aspired. She and Luther dated for several years in an up-and-down relationship that veered close to marriage before a final bitter breakup.

Encouraged by Saul in the aftermath of the split, Luther attended a few church services and was surprised by the nostalgic comfort he found. Holding a hymnal, sharing a wooden pew, singing in unison with other worshippers. It was simple and decent. This was how he'd been raised.

Luther learned of an opening to host a late-night, radio call-in show. The producers wanted hard-hitting commentary on current events and the ability to mix it up with callers. Luther made inquiries. Though attracted by his name recognition, the producers were turned off by his lack of experience. Give us a sample "churn", they said, using the industry term for the initial segment wherein the listening audience is either successfully hooked or wriggles free. Let's see what you can do with a variety of topics, they said. Info-tain us.

Luther sketched out ideas, themes, ways of presentation. He filled pages with notes, writing, rearranging. He procrastinated for days—he needed more time to get it just right. Then a producer called: they'd heard from other candidates and wanted to make a decision. Where was his sample tape, his churn?

Next morning Luther drove to a strip mall in which he was part owner. He looked the place over, listened to the retailers' complaining, picked up a portable tape recorder from Radio Shack and a crab sandwich at the deli. At home he read the paper as he munched his lunch. He went to the living room and drew the blinds. He poured himself a Chivas, placing it on the coffee table next to the recorder and a stop watch. He set the watch, pushed the recorder's red button, took a swallow of the Chivas, leaned forward and let it go:

"So I'm on the Santa Domingo Freeway on my way into the studio and it's a parking lot, we're simply not moving and next to me is a carpool lane like a desert island. Has anyone had this kind of surreal experience?

"You're deadlocked, gridlocked, absolutely landlocked and a blood clot is growing in your brain the size of a watermelon. And once in a while in this wide-open lane right next to you a Volvo tottles by with a Mondale sticker or maybe there's a Japanese car put together by robot people in robot factories and you have to be five feet tall to drive it or your head sticks out through the roof like Dino the dinosaur in Fred Flintstone. Who was a pretty decent guy by the way.

"Some folks will say Fred is what they call a patriarch. Interesting word, patriarch. Patriarchy. It's supposed to mean, the way I understand it, that old white men are running things. As opposed to old white women. That would be matriarchy and that's apparently okay.

"So you drive that stretch of road, from Santa Domingo to LAX, and you know that some social engineer thought up this whole scheme. He wants the world to be a certain way—the way he thinks it should be—*he wants to impose his values on us.* So he decides for a carpool lane.

"Why does he do this? To save the North Valencian garter snake from extinction. That's the reason. Because God forbid we would lose the North Valencian garter snake. I don't know what I'd do without mine. I have one as a pet and I take him out every night. For walks to the garter snake park. Play fetch the dead mouse. Sure. I haven't trained him to get the morning paper yet because once he's on the sidewalk, he tends to lay there and sun himself. And then I have to play fetch the garter snake.

"And nobody elected this guy, this self-important bureaucrat, this social engineer. Let's call him J. Rottenheimer Bureaucrat III. He's not accountable to anyone. Even though he cooks up this lousy idea, awful idea, does J. Rottenheimer Bureaucrat III get fired?

"No. You can't fire these people. Their unions are too strong. The union reps meet during the work day to figure out how to make the jobs more secure. And we pay for it. You and I.

"What are some of the values they want to impose on us? *Sensitivity* is one. A while back there was a little mix-up between me and a young actress. And a mediator—a court-appointed mediator—advised me I should undergo *sensitivity training.* Okay? I wasn't sensitive enough. They can train you to be sensitive to what they want you to be sensitive to, if you follow me.

"Here are some other values we're supposed to share with people that have nothing better to do than clog up our crosswalks: how about *vibrant gay community?* I'm not sure we want to have a gay community at all but I am sure I don't want it vibrating.

"Or Universal Humanism. Good grief, I used to dress up and play space invader when I was a kid, you know, with a plastic ray gun and I'd hide behind the rosemary bush and Mom would give me the dickens but I didn't keep thinking and talking that way when I got to be an adult. Crazy stuff. Weird stuff. Yet we take it for granted now like background noise on an elevator or at the ocean.

"We've allowed this for so long, the belief there are no absolute truths, that whatever fashionable theory happens to be floating around in the garden at a point in time, then that becomes the *truth du jour.*

"You walk into a classroom now—I know because I've done it—and see children taught man is an accident of nature, an evolving animal. There is no God. Only blind causation. No one plus nothing, times random chance, equals everything. That's the new math our children are learning. Doesn't add up very well, does it?

"You can talk about Captain Condom all you want but say the name Jesus Christ and see what happens. The patrol cars show up. The paddy wagon.

"A high school principal admitted to me over drinks the other night—she's an able and attractive administrator by the way—more than a third of her graduating seniors have or expect to have in a very short time, a venereal disease. I didn't ask which ones but there aren't that many to choose from. And these were the graduates!

"It's a brave new world folks. Orwell saw it coming. There's so much I want to talk about in the coming weeks. Ronald Reagan and his legacy after this so-called Iran-Contra scandal the press is cooking up. The coming threat from Japan and believe me, whatever you've heard, the truth is a whole lot scarier. And the real facts on the nuclear freeze. And hey, don't get me started on those garter snakes. I'll take your calls after this commercial message. You're listening to Luther's Nation."

He leaned back, spent. It had been boiling inside, needing release.

Now it was on this tape. He placed the tape in an envelope and searched for his car keys so he could drop it at the studio.

He poured a quick Chivas and ran his eyes round the room, wanting to remember everything about this moment: the horrible curtains, the picture of he and Saul holding up a marlin, the stuffed panda in a corner left by that stewardess. She said she'd come back for it but she never did.

He opened the blinds: light flooded in. He opened the windows: the sounds of a neighborhood afternoon, rising and falling, the most ordinary kind of music. He dug deep behind a cushion to fish out his keys and made his way out to his car in the driveway.

Luther got the job and Luther's Nation caught on. This was the Reagan era. The country was in the mood for a plain-spoken voice that was neither college professor nor pundit. In a padded chair with an irregular squeak, under a broken ceiling fan in a tee shirt and head set with notes and highlighted articles in neat piles before him, Luther stated his views and gave his reasons.

Syndicated across the wide country, Luther's Nation inspired fan clubs of the same name, each new chapter noted with a colored pin stuck in a map of the US taped to the studio wall. With a nudge now and then from the Precepts Corporation, Luther Dorsey was transformed from minor celebrity to public thinker, a figure of gravitas sought out for his views and opinions.

"Let those who know what they're doing take care of politics?" asked Luther. "We can't think like that any more. The people who know what they're doing are the ones sitting next to you Sunday mornings."

One night a caller said, "Keep putting the good word out there, Luther. Maybe some day we on the right will be able to make our voices heard."

"Thanks. I do this because I love it."

"Wanted your take on the President's statement this week that his heart told him he hadn't traded arms for hostages, but the facts and evidence said he had."

Luther said, "Frankly, I thought Reagan was too accommodating there. If I have to choose between Ronald Reagan's heart and the facts and evidence, it's no contest. Reagan feels so much for the hostages and their families and you know, those feelings and those families are part of the facts and evidence too.

"As for encouraging the kidnappers, it was not an intentional encouragement. So his moral stance on this is unstained. Unknowing and unstained, I think, sums it up. Thanks for the call and tune in tomorrow night when my guest will be a scientist who thinks the earth is getting warmer, and that you and I are the cause."

Luther interviewed the author of *They're Coming to Get You*. Once they get you, Luther pressed him, where will they take you? The author hadn't thought that far ahead. Luther chatted with a short-tempered man claiming Jesus could not have been a Jew since his last name was Christ, so that by definition He was Christian. Luther spoke with Dr. Anthony Noondale, author of *On Our Own: Adrift in a Silent Universe*. He asked the unbelieving doctor if there was such a thing as too much education.

"I'm not sure what you mean."

"Surveys show the more educated a person becomes, in the social sciences and humanities especially, the more likely he is to be an atheist. I ask again, how much education is enough?"

"Your question seems to presuppose being an atheist to be a bad thing," Noondale observed.

"Isn't it?"

"Obviously I don't think so. Since I am one."

"At least you admit to it. Tell me Dr. Noondale, do you have any children?"

"No."

"Neither do I, but every parent I know is anxious to provide religious instruction for their child. They don't want atheist teachers and firemen and bank tellers. And porn shops on every corner."

"Then I think you have to ask yourself if you want a free society at all," sniffed Noondale.

"That's precisely what we're asking for. The freedom to have a society with no atheists."

"We seem to be talking past each other."

"The Bible tells us God has made foolish the wisdom of this world. You might ponder those words, Dr. Noondale. I hope you'll join us again soon."

Success did not bring personal fulfillment. Luther felt alone in Santa Domingo. Saul Blomberg had moved to New York, to better straddle the twin empires of politics and entertainment. Women came and went. In a corner of the living room the stuffed panda bear remained, Luther still with only a vague recollection of who had left it. Exactly what it symbolized he wasn't sure.

Though given to on-air outbursts of religious fervor, Luther attended church only sporadically. Sunday mornings managed to fill up with golf outings and sailing. Sometimes there were business trips, more and more often, hangovers.

The routine of daily radio began to grind; callers started to sound the same. Luther became more demanding, more ideological and therefore less tolerant when their views diverged from his own.

"Here's a phrase you don't ever hear from the mainstream media," he said one night. "Moral degenerate. Why not? Because their darling is one. Yes, the President of the United States is a moral degenerate, I'm sad to report. He's had extramarital affairs. He demonstrated against his own country. In a foreign land. In a time of war. And the last thing our popular President wants is to get any of his conquests pregnant, I assure you. So here, I'll pick up this call and hang it back up because it's irrelevant. I know what they'll say. The GNP is up and we're not at war, so why are you complaining? Here's my answer: a nation is judged not by its GNP or lack of wars. It's judged by the virtue of its leaders. That's a little secret they don't want you to know."

Late one night, sky blurry with stars, Luther drove along a slender Malibu canyon road, eyes bleary from booze. Failing to negotiate a hairpin turn, his midnight-colored Eradicator tore through an overmatched guard rail and his plunge toward the canyon floor was interrupted only by the fortuitous placement of a scrub oak, in whose venerable, widespreading branches Luther found himself entangled seconds later: nearly upside down, a cut above his left eye, his right shin throbbing, his heart racing like a hunted animal.

He slowly worked free of the vehicle, careful not to dislodge it from the branches that had served as his salvation. At daybreak back up on the winding road, he hailed a ride from a startled starlet driving in early to a studio to shoot a disaster flick.

Our existence is fleeting. Reactions can vary to such an epiphany. Another foot to the left or right, the tow truck driver informed him with a frankly appraising lift of his cap, and you'd be pushing up the posies.

Luther pronounced himself born again, this time in the Spirit. He would enroll in divinity school. His life henceforth would be dedicated to the God of the Bible Who had created him and saved him for purposes only He knew but which Luther had no doubt were significant.

His conversion was reported with wry amusement by the press and the tabloid news shows. The role of alcohol in the accident was rarely omitted. Old footage of his now-campy White Sail ads was resurrected, along with barbs about being in the right place at the right time or hitting the right tree at the right time. Ninety percent of life, it was chuckled, was just showing up.

Luther's Nation continued but with a more God-centered focus. A segment was added called *A Walk Down Skid Row*, wherein Luther took his microphones to LA's alleyways and shooting galleries to talk with the bums and junkies and shopping cart pushers.

One such outing Luther came upon a crouching man better cared for, better dressed than the rest in his comfy, relaxed-fit jeans. A man with an obvious intelligence coupled to a peculiar mixture of caution and resolve, as of a mind on the verge of an apprehension it would greatly regret and so is determined not to make. He had pale, watery eyes and a ginger mustache that lay across his upper lip like the business end of a toothbrush. He would swipe a tiny mustache comb through this ginger mustache when he thought he could get away with it.

The man recited his tale: a child prodigy reared in the perpetual sunshine of Orange County; a distinguished academic career culminating in a doctorate in organizational psychology from the University of Santa Rita, one of the nation's first for-profit universities. He'd become radicalized during the student protests of the late '60's, even once leading a spontaneous march to the home of the university president, which proved a disappointment since the only address the protesters had was the P.O. Box where they sent their tuition checks.

There followed a drift into EST, then an untenured teaching position at a junior college, the downward spiral culminating with an ill-timed acquisition of a realtor's license as the southern California housing market made its end-of-Cold-War plunge. He wasn't an alcoholic or even homeless. Just a regular listener whose life was broken and needed to be fixed.

"What's keeping you from fixing it?" asked Luther.

The man gave a hopeless sigh.

"Throw a stone up a thousand times and it still falls back to earth. That's the law of nature."

"Unless God wills it not to be so."

"Why would He do that for me?"

Luther said, "Arise, Max Winter."

"How do you know my name?" Max answered, rising in obedience and giving a wondering swipe to his ginger mustache.

"The Lord has told me of you," said Luther with a showman's disregard for the truth since it was his producer who had told him just before they went on air.

From that night Max Winter was devoted to Luther, starting as an unpaid intern around the studio, running errands at first, then taking on more complex assignments.

He had his quirks, which Luther soon grew fond of. Max spurned coffee as unhealthy, neckties as illogical. He abhorred calico cats and said newspapers were relics of the past. A bond grew between the two; at first it was Max leaning on Luther's outer strength and social power and position. But then as Luther allowed Max to be the good friend he had missed since Saul Blomberg moved away, it was Luther who became more confiding, more in need of a friend's empathy and understanding.

Luther still spoke frequently with Saul. He complained to Saul that he wanted to do more, make more of an impact. He said he was ready for something different, but didn't know exactly what.

Saul put out some feelers and he called Luther one evening about an opportunity. It would be a fresh start. Might lead to big, big things. It would require relocation to the south, the New South. A well-positioned mega-church had embarked on a nationwide search for a high-profile pastor to lead them into the new millennium. Luther and Saul talked into the early morning.

That night Luther bade farewell to his long-time listeners, explaining that the Lord was calling him. Perhaps, depending on His plan, they would be hearing from him in the future. He had a feeling they would.

Luther was about to re-make himself, yet again, and it made him proud. Of all the gifts America offers, he thought, this is the greatest: that we can change who we are by a simple act of will.

TWENTY
YEARS LATER

III

"FREEDOM FRIES WITH THAT SHAKE?"

Her eyes are round and shallow, like a petri dish. Her cheeks are marred with minor eruptions, pink and temporary but experienced as eternal. She inhabits a crinkly uniform, her head is adorned with a crinkly hat and logo: a blue hen grinning half-knowing, half-maniacal, and the hen itself adorned with a fire engine-red halo beneath a flourishing script that reads: *Dorsey's Temple of Chicken.*

Roland Orr grins back, more at the hen than the girl waiting for his answer.

"Freedom fries?" she repeats dutifully. "Dollar forty-nine. All profits are tithed to support our troops in…in…" She whispers to a co-worker and receives a whisper in return.

"The greater Caspian Sea region," she concludes in triumph.

"Just the shake." Roland holds out a five.

"Sorry. That isn't Dorseys. You have to pay in Dorseys."

"Don't have Dorseys. Just this. See? Lincoln."

She shakes her head.

"We've built monuments to this man," Roland says. "He freed the slaves. Held the country together. You can't turn him away."

She recites from memory: "All foodstuffs and merchandise vended on the grounds of the Praiseful Worship Everlasting Gospel Church complex must be paid for in Dorseys, purchasable at the main entrance or from any of numerous conveniently located ticket booths."

Not looking up she points to a sign above her head and smiles, sort of.

Roland returns a grin of his own, the one that used to wow the girls.

"This is legal tender, my tender one. I'd like a shake. Por favor. S'il vous plait. Si se puede."

She rolls her eyes. What a showoff. And the line growing behind him, if noted, will drag down her PPP (Praiseful Power Performance rating). She speaks to her headset in quiet urgency.

A side door opens, a manager-trainee emerges. He is courteous but firm: no Dorseys, no shake. Roland, equally courteous, is equally firm: no shakee, no leavee.

The manager-trainee is not sure what to make of this particular challenge to his customer service skills. Roland has a careless quality, an indifference to the sensibilities of those surrounding him. Yet at the same time a reserve, a holding-back, as if watching himself. As if observing his own fall from grace.

"The baby Jesus was turned away from the inn and had to sleep in a manger," says Roland. "He also lacked the required Dorseys."

At this odious comparison several Temple of Chicken associates abandon posts to confront Roland with gleaming eyes. Amid the melee the manager-trainee notices a man on the tiny lawn out back pointing a cell phone as if taping the scene within. That would be a breach of security, an orange alert. The main office must be notified.

Soon an electric-powered golf cart glides to a stop outside. A well-built woman in a pantsuit one size too small disembarks to assess the situation and enters the Temple of Chicken.

"Jefferson rewrote the New Testament," Roland is declaiming, as if following a script. "He removed the miracles because he didn't believe they happened. Without miracles there's only parables. And suffering."

The pants suit is now before him, frowning, hands on hips.

"What's your point?"

"Anyone can make up parables," Roland answers.

"Why don't you make one up, then?"

"A stranger presents himself at the inn, thirsting for refreshment. But he's turned away. Why?"

"That sounds more like a riddle than a parable."

"Best I could do on short notice."

"Who are you?" she asks, no longer amused.

"A seeker after shakes. And you?"

She has the impression he already knows who she is.

"I'm Blaze Dorsey," she says, in cool appraisal of his designer sunglasses and too-hip demeanor. "Luther Dorsey's wife, if that helps. Why is this being filmed?"

"That guy could be anybody," Roland answers, jerking his thumb outside.

"You just happen to be passing through a private church complex followed by a man videotaping you as you cause a childish disturbance? Why don't I believe you?"

"Only you can answer that Blaze. Is it all right if I call you Blaze?"

"Thanks for asking. No. Here's how this will work. You leave now or you're escorted off the grounds, no shake included and by the way, that fellow you don't know out there just had his cell phone confiscated and he'll be leaving with you."

"I'm offering to pay."

"You're a disturbance."

"Sometimes people need to be disturbed."

Blaze hits speed dial. Local police arrive to remove the cooperating Roland Orr from the premises. She watches as he's handcuffed and a cop holds his head down, forcing him into the backseat. It all goes smoothly.

Blaze Cornsilk had six brothers, but was the only daughter of an Air Force chaplain and a former Miss Oklahoma. Blaze herself had entered several beauty contests as a young woman, winning some renown in the finals of the Miss USA Talent Competition when she rendered the Sermon on the Mount in American Sign Language while balancing on a unicycle and eating an apple. One day on a whim she tried out to be one of the high-kicking Dallas Cowboy cheerleaders. Selected for the squad, she used that platform to carve out a niche as a fitness model and Christian aerobics instructor ("Fat cells are the Devil's workshop!").

Luther, during one of his increasingly frequent sleepless nights, spotted her in an infomercial for a teeth-brightening product and requested a meeting through her agent. They married within months in a surprisingly understated ceremony. Max Winter was Luther's best man, the two sharing a wide-ranging discussion of the female psychology in the rectory of the Episcopal Diocese in north Dallas as the ceremony was delayed so Blaze could do some last-minute crunches.

Blaze is going to mention the strange incident to Luther at dinner but in the middle of chopping celery for a salad, she hears local news give the name of the arrested man as Roland Orr. She stops mid-chop. Luther had spoken often of a childhood friend, a Roland. There were stories Luther told about he and Roland, and Blaze had often thought Luther looked happier when he told them than at any other time.

She darts to a closet in the storage space beneath the stairs, digs up a shoe box holding mementos of Luther's past. There's a letter or two in Roland's loopy script, and some tiny black and whites of Luther and Roland, skinny kids in buzz cuts looking quizzically at the picture-taker. Luther has that same happy look.

Blaze had figured out soon enough that Luther, for all the bulked-up strength of his persuasive exterior, could be sensitive to life's setbacks, wanting things to be perfect, more and more let down each time he discovered anew that they were not. She had appointed herself to the job of filtering disappointment and surprise out of Luther's world.

She learns of Roland Orr's sentence: ten days on a road crew laying asphalt for willful interference in the functioning of a religious establishment. Yes'm, sheriff says, he'll be wearing the stripes.

She's waiting outside the day of Roland's release. Roland wanders out in his designer shades, denim jacket and a tee shirt with lettering that says The Evolution Will Not be Televised. Tucked under his arm he cradles a paper bag like a football, the entirety of his worldly possessions.

He sees Blaze up ahead waiting, arms akimbo, sneaking in a few lunges alongside a double-parked convertible as the ex-prisoners file past to greet their loved ones. She offers a heavy-breathing wave and a lift.

They drive to an out-of-the way restaurant where an eager waiter seats them outdoors next to a slatted trellis enveloped by a wrapping vine. The linen is crisp and white. Blaze orders her favorite sauvignon blanc—crisp and light—and mixed greens with orange slices, pecans and crumbly gorgonzola pieces she picks around. Figuring he's not paying, Roland has steak under onions and a beer.

A man is leaving the restaurant. He stops and stares at Roland, lowering his dark glasses to better see.

"You're Roland Orr," he says with the smile of a man who can't believe his good fortune. "San Diego Chargers. I was a member of your fan club. After you had that one big year."

The man seems like he's about to say something else, something more personal, but he stops. "Can I get an autograph?" he asks. "For my nephew."

"Sure, pal," says a pleased Roland, scribbling his signature on a napkin.

Blaze arches her eyebrows. "You have your own fan club?"

"Wish I still did," says Roland. "Never underestimate how good it feels to have your own fan club. Mine only lasted a couple years. Then it fell apart pretty quick."

"You must have been quite a player."

"I was a flanker," he says, the memories flooding back to him. "They threw the ball and I chased it down and caught it. That was all I had to do. Powder blue uniform, lightning bolt on my helmet. Forty thousand fans in the stands. There were times in the summer, in the evening when we were doing passing drills, the clouds would roll in from the ocean and cool things down and I felt like I could run forever. I never thought life could be that good."

"What happened?"

"What do you mean?"

"That guy just now, the fan. He said you had that one big year."

"I did," insists Roland. "I did have that one big year."

"That was all? Just one?

He becomes interested in finishing his beer. She changes the subject.

"When did you last see Luther?"

"In person? Not since the 60's," Roland says with a laugh at how Time tries to trick us into thinking we've grown old.

"That long? He talks about you. I thought you had been more in touch. Were you in Vietnam?"

"I was in the army but not Vietnam. They sent me to Spain. I played on a general's football team. He needed a flanker. Crazy world huh?"

Blaze nods in swift agreement. "We were in Europe several years ago. Rome. Luther met with one of the cardinals."

"Only time I was in Rome we ate hash brownies in the morning with a double espresso and spent the day pretending we were street mimes." He has a way of talking fast then stopping with a wide-eyed look, as if to ascertain his effect. She takes out cigarettes, offers one; he says he doesn't smoke tobacco. She lights up with a cross of bare legs and a frank expression.

Roland says, "When I stopped playing pro, I heard my old sergeant was acting on some pictures back in Spain. Spaghetti westerns. He got me a part so then I did that for a while."

She grants him the favor of her smile. "I'll bet you were the leading man."

"Sure, once. Movie called *The Sun Won't Go Down*."

He signals for a refill. "Mind if I get one more?"

"You have a habit of asking permission after you've already done something."

"My name was Ringo," he continues. "I went after these guys who stole my favorite gun, the one my dad gave me as he lay dying. Got 'em one by one. Last guy had my dad's gun. I wrestled it away and he was cowering in the corner holding up both hands like this, begging me not to shoot. I pulled the trigger anyway. It didn't go off though, it wasn't loaded. That's how I learned to not trust guns and trust people instead. At least that's what they told me. That was my biggest role. Eventually I came back to the States and coached."

"Football again?"

"Yeah, high school. That was pretty much all I knew."

"Luther played football too, didn't he?"

"Oh yeah, Luther was a big boy and he got a real emotion going about some games, some of the big games. When he was motivated nobody could stop him."

Blaze swells with pride. Then she remembers something else Luther had said about Roland.

"Yeah," he admits. "I got busted. Then I got fired and couldn't find coaching work after that. Everywhere I applied I got turned down. Philadelphia. Tacoma. In Boise, Idaho I show up first day of practice, they pull me aside, tell me certain revelations have come up about my past."

"But I'm clean now," he adds almost as an afterthought. He catches the waiter's eye, indicating his empty glass.

"What kind of drugs was it?" Blaze wants to know.

"Kind of old-fashioned. Never caught on over here."

She's already learned she can wait him out.

"I'd rather not talk about it," he says, reddening. "It's something people were doing over there in Europe at the time. You know, actors. That crowd."

She's found another weakness.

She says, "I'm sorry about the other day but you were so obnoxious. Why?"

He chooses his words carefully. "I guess you'd say it's a developmental thing. I don't know what to say about it. I'm not supposed to say anything."

"But if it involves Luther, I need to know."

"Luther knows about it. I think. I don't know. He *will* know about it."

"Why was it being taped?"

"You have to trust me on that one."

"How can I trust you? I don't know you. Is there a camera on us now?"

"Wouldn't be surprised. Don't worry, you look great."

She lights another cigarette and they eye each other as his compliment hangs in the air. He has a friendly face, perhaps a little too boyish when he smiles, and unruly hair in dark-blonde clumps. Dirt under his nails from the road gang. Deadpan expression, eyes darting away if she looks too close or too long.

He senses she's evaluating him, wondering why he's popped up all of a sudden. He also senses disapproval, a reaction he seems to engender more and more these days.

"I'm not asking for myself," she says. "Luther is very vulnerable now. Coming so close like he did in the last election. To actually being the President…"

"Not to be cruel but he didn't come that close."

"Up until Ohio it looked like we might win. Luther was making plans, what he would do the first hundred days. Hiring lists, things like that. You have to be prepared. You have to believe. When the voters turned away, he didn't understand. He still doesn't."

"People like politicians the way they like pop music," Roland says, pleased with this observation.

Now Blaze is remembering. "The things that influence voters, that they tell you influence voters. It's the strangest process to be part of. All these people telling you how you're being seen by people you can't see."

She reaches for the cigarettes, stops. "Vietnam. Of all things. How many wars have we had since then? And he supported every one."

She's rapping the table for emphasis. Roland has found a weakness, too.

The meal is over. He puts on his denim jacket. "Don't worry about the camera and all that. You'll be hearing from this guy soon. He has a funny name. Evor Lark. He'll explain everything."

They're at her car. "Want a ride?" she asks, eyeing herself in the rear-view.

"Thanks, think I'll stretch my legs." Blaze backs out the convertible.

Across the street a shopping mall beckons, even to a man with little to spend but time. An ill-considered dash leaves Roland stranded briefly on a median strip planted in ginkgo trees all in a row, fan-shaped leaves flickering in the lingering, spring light. A police car cruises by, double-chinned officer wagging a finger of warning. The traffic passes.

In the mall Roland wanders, consumed by the feeling of freedom, ordering coffee in the heady atmosphere of a super-grande-bookstore café. He browses the shelves, thinking of his impending reunion with Luther. Best friend as kids. But forty years later…and Luther a big-time pastor and presidential candidate.

Roland chooses from among the colorful volumes, *God for Dummies* by Dr. Anthony Noondale, and he settles into a cushioned chair chosen for the view it affords of the slender baristas laboring among the percolation vats.

Roland reads the book's first sentence: "The Jehovah of ancient Israel was a fusion of the many gods the nomadic nation had encountered in years of wandering."

Author's pretty sure of himself, thought Roland. He flips ahead. 'Jehovah is a jealous God. Irked by the refusal of the Amalekites to worship Him, He had them cast into fiery pits and forced others to stand on a single leg, wearing hoods. 'That Freedom Foy God' is the ungrammatical translation of an inscription found on one Amalekitian tomb.'

Sounds familiar, thinks Roland. He reads further, a passage from Genesis, just after Adam and Eve become aware they are naked:

> *"They heard the sound of the Lord God moving about in the garden at the breezy time of day; and the man and his wife hid from the Lord God among the trees of the garden. The Lord God called out to the man and said to him, "Where are you?"*

Why, asked the author Noondale, does the Lord God have to ask where Adam is? Does He not know all, see all? Or is God playing with Adam, as a cat with its prey?

Roland grows thoughtful, not suspicious as the author Noondale intends. Instead Roland is moved by the image of the searching Lord calling out as the evening settles in, seeking a friend to make the coming night less lonely: "Where are you?" Roland develops an odd sympathy for Jehovah, who after all has no friends, no wife, no hobbies other than his disobedient creatures.

No mother or father.

Jehovah strikes Roland as insecure, irritable. Angered by the actions of his toy soldiers, sometimes moved to knock them over. Such ferocious punishment meted out for so mild a sin. A bitten piece of fruit. Why give man the capacity to sin, then be angered when he does? Why make His own existence uncertain, then punish those who don't believe?

"We are men and should think like men," wrote Noondale, delivering his closing verdict on the final page. "There are no gods in our past and none in our future. The sooner we face up to this, the better."

Closing the book Roland looks again at its cover, realizing he'd misread the title, which was actually *God Is for Dummies*. No wonder he'd found it among the sloppy piles on the bargain table. He stays until the store closes, paying for refills at a discounted price and removing books from the shelves to skim through and then put back; he leaves without buying any.

* * * * * *

It is April, which is the cruelest month, but it is a Friday, one of the kinder days. We are in midtown Manhattan. For this single moment pretend we no longer are bound by restrictions of natural law. Instead we are like the indolent gods afloat, held up by currents of air, buoyed by motionless breeze. And we've chosen at this moment to place ourselves on these invisible pillows in this eternal repose amid the stalwart skyscrapers thrusting defiantly up all around us.

We are gods; we are bored. Eternity tends to have that effect. We are gods; we are voyeurs. Immortality tends to have that effect. So we amuse ourselves by peering in these glass-encased tombs to observe the doings of these fragile, glass-encased mortals.

We find in one particular penthouse boardroom an immaculate, climate-less comfort with which we are simpatico. A truly global outlook is here expressed: ergonomic chairs assembled by striving Taiwanese, carpet woven by grateful Guatemalans, water in the cooler arriving daily at outlandish expense from Icelandic springs. We are at the home office of the Precepts Corporation.

Evor Lark traces a slender finger along a conference table's freshly-waxed surface, breathing in its perfumy fragrance. It occurs to him what an admirable thing wood is, how effortlessly it evokes character and tradition.

Lark's frame is slight and unrevealing. A meager head of hair, blonde from a bottle on the advice of a high-priced stylist who said do something creative while you still have some left. His eyes, an unimpeachable blue, have settled in atop two chubby cheeks which may one day turn jowly, but for now evoke an unformed potential. People who make it their business to know say Evor Lark is an ascending player, that if he can do a turn-around on the Luther Dorsey account his status will be sealed as successor to the soon-to-retire Saul Blomberg.

Evor is calm on the verge of his greatness. He makes a minimal glance at his multi-display wrist watch; he's expecting Luther's chief of staff, Max Winter. There is a swooshing sound and the doors part and in walks Max.

Once-lost, once-drifting Max. His unease with the world and his place in it replaced now with a vital feeling: that he has something to contribute through his connection to Luther Dorsey. Over the years Max has cemented his position as Luther's right-hand man, second-in-command, chief tactician, in-house intellectual and sometimes late-night confidante during his leader's spiritual crises.

Next enters the balding, avuncular Saul Blomberg, Luther's old friend from the California days. Saul has aged but has retained his sharp eyes and California tan. He sits across from Max, with Evor Lark by his side. Evor's personal assistant Desmond, drooping eyes invariably dripping with a private amusement, sits shoulders hunched at the far end of the table behind a lap top and projector, gliding below the collective radar.

Saul flips the speaker phone on at center table and Luther's baritone emerges: "—root beer and a jumbo bag of cheese fritters. Here's a five. I expect change. Oh hey is this thing on? Saul? Max? Everybody there?"

"Luther!"

"Big Luth!"

"I'm here too!" Blaze's voice also emerges from the speaker phone.

There is a pause. Saul occupies the vacuum.

"Luther, Blaze, we're sorry you couldn't make it today but we think we have an exciting idea to present and since we're all busy people, without further adieu if you'll pardon the expression, I'll turn it over to one of our young vice-presidents with a brilliant future in this business and some great ideas to present. And who also happens to be a heckuva nice guy. Evor Lark."

Evor rises. His manner is clinical yet enthusiastic, like a male yell leader performing an autopsy.

"I'll begin by saying what an honor it is to possibly—hopefully—work with a man who has done so many great things and who came so close to, well, being President of the United States."

"So close!" Blaze's voice echoes.

Evor continues. "Let's do some triage. The patient is Luther Dorsey. Fifty-something white male. Heartbreaking loss in the last presidential primary. Pastor of a commercially and spiritually successful mega-church. Former governor. Best-selling author. Strong, strong name recognition. Strong, strong charitable record both at home and in the international arena. Exceptional speaking style, able to move crowds both in person and via digital media. Mailing lists to die for and still has a pretty full head of hair, which never hurts.

Evor pauses for a drink of water. Eight glasses a day.

"Now let's have a closer look at that presidential run. We found positive associations in voter's minds between Luther Dorsey and personal freedom, Luther Dorsey and protecting the homeland, Luther Dorsey and proximity to the Creator of all that surrounds us. The patient's fatal flaw can be summarized in a single word: "character.""

From the speakerphone: "Ouch."

"Luther your overall package is formidable," Saul says quickly. "We may need to do a little restoration, scrape off the debris so the true Luther can shine through. Like they do with any masterpiece."

"Drinks? Pastries?" Lark offers brightly, indicating a wheeled-in tray.

The tray is left untouched. Max removes a pack of peppermint gum, offering a stick to Saul. The discomfort in the room is palpable. Thoughts have gone back to the Ohio primary, which would have been Luther's first win in a northern state and have lent to the campaign a much-needed aura of legitimacy.

Polls had looked good, buoyed by Luther's celebrated put-down to a visiting dignitary that "my God can kick your God's ass."

The tide began to turn on an attack ad featuring a clip of Mussolini addressing the Italian people in the early days of television. The strutting dictator, who shared with Luther a prominent jaw line as well as other superficial mannerisms, was speaking directly into the camera and as Mussolini's mouth moved, viewers of the attack ad heard Luther's voice giving what at the time had been a well-received address to the annual convention of the Veterans of Preventative Wars. By an unhappy coincidence, Luther's speech had argued forcefully for an invasion of Ethiopia.

Then came more trouble over a resume distributed by a low-level campaign volunteer claiming Luther had "seen a lot of action" during Vietnam. Confronted by reporters over Luther's lack of military service, the Dorsey campaign could only offer the lame explanation that the reference was to Luther's TV viewing.

The press had a field day. Luther was labeled a "chickenhawk"—eager to engage the US in war but none too eager to personally serve. The chickenhawk association was aided in no small part by an existing identity in voter's minds between Luther and the grinning hen logo of his ubiquitous Temple of Chicken franchises.

Luther lost Ohio by twenty points. Then came yet another mishap: the misspelling of "recycle" for a precocious Wisconsin fourth-grader. And in the frantic, final days before the polls closed in California, Luther committed the cardinal sin of campaigning: attempting to kiss two babies at once he allowed one of the suspiciously over-powdered infants to slip from his grasp.

Luther's post-defeat depression lasted far longer than doctors thought it should. He grew a beard, shaved it, put on weight, had it removed, put it back on, took up power-walking to get his competitive juices flowing, even trying roller-blading once before giving a bad twist to an ankle.

It was Max who initiated a dialogue with Precepts, hoping to light a fire under his spiritless leader. Thus far Luther had remained tepid to all entreaties, as evidenced by his phoned-in presence at this morning's meeting.

Evor concluded his introductory remarks.

"Luther is a great American. Like many great Americans he is a maligned American. We need to show personal qualities of bravery and integrity. The kind of man people want to follow. And it wouldn't hurt if the whole thing is done with a little environmental sensitivity."

"Fine," says Max, who's given himself an orange juice mustache, "so what do we do?"

Saul nods to Evor, who signals Desmond, who fingers a button.

Shades lower. Lights dim. Evor begins a thoughtful pacing.

"What is an American?" he asks. "What is unique about America? Not our form of government. There are other constitutions. Other democracies. Even Europe has them.

"I ask if there is not a deeper truth, a prior experience, more fundamental than the Founding Fathers. More uniquely American. I'm thinking of the Puritans. The Puritan experience is the seminal American experience. It reaches to the roots of our national psyche and is an underutilized source of national identity and pride.

"Who then were the Puritans? Underdogs. They crossed an ocean in tiny vessels, threatened by shipwreck and disease. They had to be shown how to plant corn. They battled the wilderness and starvation and hostile natives. In many different ways they waged war on superior forces.

"Now let's think about warfare at this moment in our history. The market for it is saturated. 'Too many wars' comes up again and again in our polling. 'I lost my son.' 'I lost a neighbor.' 'My child's teacher is dead.'

"A new way is needed. A way for a candidate to emulate the Puritans. Demonstrate his bravery, integrity and faith. In the role of an underdog, with the trappings of war but without actually waging war."

From modest but powerful speakers comes the sound of trumpets: muted, filled with longing, unafraid.

"What if we could fuse Luther's personal destiny to the country's as a whole—while he's not even holding office!—by having him lead a diverse group of Americans on an adventure of heroic proportions?

"Cue the violins," Lark commands. Lush strings invoke the solemnity of distant vistas.

An image projects onto a lowered screen: the ocean's waves, the unending sea. Words are superimposed: 'U.S.S. UnderGod.' They fade, replaced by a sailing ship: tall, draped in chalky-white canvas. A flag flaps from the mizzenmast in stripes of red and white and a corner-square of navy blue populated not by stars but a circle of crosses. Below the flag: black-tarred rigging, varnished railing, polished brass work. Snub-nosed carronades peek from the upper deck portholes, and from the decks below the menacing thrust of the twenty-four-pounders, the long guns. Off the bow a figurehead carved into the oaken hull: an eagle clutching in its talons two crossed arrows as it scans the horizon for enemies with a gaze both fierce and uncomprehending.

"Gentlemen," Evor continues. "This is the U.S.S. UnderGod. A meticulous reconstruction of a nineteenth-century frigate of the United States Navy, the current property of a group of patriotic naval retirees and Mexican War enthusiasts. The UnderGod is being offered for sale at a price substantially below retail and the Precepts Corporation has obtained an exclusive option to purchase over the next thirty days.

"Our proposal is nothing less than this," Larks says, his grip tightening on his laser pointer just a little. "At a time when America is being urged to withdraw, stand down, to mind our own business, we propose the UnderGod be sailed under God Almighty and the leadership of Captain Luther B. Dorsey"—the ship morphed now into a map of the globe and Lark's pointer went to work—"out the Beaufort, South Carolina harbor, down the South American coast, around Cape Horn and across the Pacific past this little dot here which is called Christmas Island—how great is that?—then across this other ocean, around the Horn of Africa through the southern Atlantic back to the harbor in Beaufort. From where—"

"Evor! I love it!" Blaze's voice leaps into the room.

"Blaze! Let me finish!" Lark protests. "From where, minutes after it docks with what we expect to be saturation media coverage Luther announces he will again seek his party's nomination to be President of the United States."

"We can do this Luther!" Blaze again. "We can do this!"

Cymbals crash, then sizzle to silence.

"We?" says Luther, weakly.

"Let's not get carried away," says Max. "We need to hear a lot more detail."

"Absolutely," says Saul. "That's why we're here. Evor, great presentation. Let's open up to questions from Team Dorsey.

"When do we sail?" asks Blaze.

"Whoa! We're getting way ahead of ourselves," says Max.

"Luther?" says Saul.

"The sea has always been kind to me."

"For starters," says Max, "Luther would be out of the public eye the entire voyage. The whole concept violates the first law of political marketing, which is to get coverage for your candidate."

"Evor?" says Saul.

"Max, I don't know how closely you follow the financial press but the Precepts Corporation last month acquired a controlling interest in the Opticon Television Network. And only this morning we concluded an agreement in principle with our global affiliates under which they will televise what we think will be the mother of all reality TV shows: The Voyage of the UnderGod."

"What's the brandscape?" Max demands.

"Desmond?" says Lark.

Desmond reads from a list: "UnderGod wine, UnderGod calendars, UnderGod flag football leagues, UnderGod underwear, coffee imported from UnderGod-approved shade tree plantations. Key chains, cologne, and an energy drink-malt liquor tentatively called UnderGrog. That's it so far."

"That cologne should do well," Luther remarks.

Max says, "I admit there's an appealing conceptual sweep to it. But doesn't it all hinge on there being an element of real danger? If the ship merely sails the globe followed by a yacht full of reporters drinking Heinekens, who's going to care?"

"Exactly," says Lark. "It would be another trashy reality show. That's why we'll have one hundred percent historical accuracy. Historically accurate food, clothing and navigational devices. No support ships. No contact with other ships of any kind. The dangers will be real. And I can name them. Disease. Shipwreck. Mutiny."

Blaze gives out a gasp.

"Remember the premise we started from," says Lark. "Luther is serious—dead serious—about another shot at the White House. How do you dislodge a sitting President during a time of wars? You have to take chances."

"Who still knows how to sail these?" says Max.

"You'd be surprised. Clubs and maritime societies in port cities all over the world do this sort of thing, though on a smaller scale."

"And the crew?"

"That's a concern I have," the speaker phone breaks in. "That the crew would be, ah, amenable to my leadership. After all as you've pointed out we wouldn't want to have a, well, mutiny on our hands."

"That's the last thing any of us wants," puts in Saul. "The crew will be fully vetted. No malcontents."

"They'll be ordinary Americans," Lark says. "From all walks of life. We'll give them a crash course in sailsmanship then off we go."

Saul says, "Luther, where are you on this?"

"I'll have to pray. Do some fasting. Listen to the Lord."

"Sounds like a great plan. Evor will stay in touch and we'll see where this idea goes. You know it's too bad you couldn't make it this morning because if you could see this ship, this UnderGod, it really is a thing of beauty."

The voice emerging from the speakerphone contains a guarded enthusiasm as it references a cherished line of movie dialogue:

"Just one more question: Do we get to win this time?"

Evor breaks into hoots: "Rambo! Rambo! Rambo!"

"That's it Luther," says Saul, intense, envisioning. "Keep that edge. Your team needs you. We all need you. Now more than ever."

The next day Saul places a private call to Luther, who has already fallen back into one of his funks.

"Didn't your spine tingle just a little at Evor's presentation?" Saul coaxes.

"That could have been my sciatica. Now I'm having doubts. So much would be out of my control."

"Luther, as an old friend I'm going to say a few things. One, this country needs you. So this isn't just about Luther Dorsey. It's about the United States of America.

"Two, your people came to us wanting to craft a new narrative. Ideally that sort of thing is done years in advance of a run for office. There's time to lay down convincing crumbs on the biographical trail. Evor's proposal is, I'll admit, condensed. But there's no other way. You need multi-level rehabilitation and you need it now. It's risky but the upside is enormous. You have to decide whether you've got the fire in the belly."

Luther gave a decidedly non-combustible sigh.

"I'll think about it, Saul."

"Talk with Evor, Luther. Get to know him. He's someone you can work with. It's a flat world now and Evor understands that, in a way I don't think you or I ever will."

The phone in Evor Lark's office rang.

"It's Mr. Dorsey."

"Put him through."

"Evor?

"Luther!"

"In the flesh. Over the phone, that is. Had an idea last night, maybe I'm crazy I don't know. Any chance we get Mel Gibson on the boat with us? Provide some spiritual insight?"

"Oh Luther. Great idea. By the way I think it's called a ship. As far as Mel, my goodness we already looked into it! But he's doing a documentary for the Discovery Channel. A Day in the Life of Satan. It just wouldn't work with the time commitment we'd require."

"Too bad. He's a man who knows how to get his point across. Well, I'm still praying and fasting."

"You must be losing weight."

"Not really. More of a binge and purge thing. Can't stay away from those spiced jerky sticks you get at the mini-mart. Blaze says they're not healthy but I love 'em."

"Fresh fruits and green, leafy vegetables, Luther. And a little ice cream for the devil inside."

"I hear you, Evor. Let's talk later this week."

Evor at his desk.

The phone.

Luther.

"Evor, are you right with the Lord? Are you rapture-ready?"

"I think so. But it's not for me to decide, is it? Each night I jump in my jammies and say a little prayer then I snuggle under the covers. Last night I asked God to guide you in your decision about the UnderGod."

"I felt that," said Luther. "I felt that intervention. 10:30-10:45?"

"Yes!"

"I was just—had turned on a DVD. Jessica Simpson cardio workout."

"Don't let Blaze catch you watching those!"

"No chance of that. She's in her room with her Masterpiece Theater. Gets up now and then to do her tai chi but I can hear the floorboards creak. Just one more thing. Can you guarantee me no nudity of any kind?"

"Absolutely."

"In writing, now."

"Done."

"No cleavage. No butt cracks. I'm sure you understand the politics."

"Luther, I'll draw up the language tonight, we'll copy Max and brown truck it to you before you're out of the shower in the morning."

"Not a shower day tomorrow," said Luther. "I'll look for it just the same. I—I'm getting to like doing business with you, son. Through you, I believe the Lord is answering every objection I raise."

"Luther! I'd love to think that! A couple of my old frat buddies tell me God has been using them like a tool! They say it's an awesome experience."

"Not always what it's cracked up to be," said Luther.

Friday nights are normally a time of quiet self-reward for Evor Lark. But tonight is special: that morning he'd flown to Luther's Beaufort Island retreat for the final signatures; Luther signed with a smile half-eager, half-pained.

Now Evor is back in his Manhattan loft, in bed wearing his favorite satin-cloth pajamas covered in an abstract pattern of candy-apple reds and poison-apple blues and a scrawled signature repeated at intervals—an illegible facsimile of an autograph the saleslady assured him was Jules Verne's. Evor's toes are twinkling, as they tend to do in his moments of triumph. He spoon-feeds himself from a bowl in his lap occupied by an enormous wedge of marshmallow cocoa-puff Nutter Buddy Peanut Huggy butter-fudge choc-o'-chip ice cream. Lo-fat.

Yet even here in this ultra-celebratory moment, Evor's getting a little work done, scanning a disc assembled by personal assistant Desmond of interviews with potential UnderGod crew members.

Suddenly Evor sits with a start—like a hunting dog on point—childish self-indulgence shoved aside by adult-like intensity. His toes accelerate into overdrive.

The DVD is showing a man supervising the painting of a mural. A sign nearby reads Central Appalachia University. Wiping at his big, friendly forehead with the sleeve of a threadbare jacket, the man gives his name as Walter Pickett. He is a down-to-earth sort with an engaging manner, but there is an almost existential uncertainty too, as if he's not sure he has a bed for the night and is about to ask if you know of any.

"Teaching assistant," he says in answer to an off-screen interviewer's question. "Whilst I pursue muh doctorate in art history."

His current mural project is a FEMA-sponsored memorial to those who died in the strife-torn weeks following the Great Gas Price Increase.

Walter states to the camera some personal details: favorite bluegrass band (New American Centurions), least favorite book of the Bible: Ruth

("Who's she? Don't even sound biblical.") His intramural volleyball team has four wins, nine losses, an unexceptional lack of success that seems somehow affecting.

"And you're studying art history. Why?"

"I reckon them ole-time artists to be a special blessin'," says Walter. "Whut with their cherubs an' angels an' whatnot. I kin gaze on a paintin' by Titian er Andrea del Sarto fer hours. Drives muh wife to distracktion, I'm sorry to say."

Do you consider yourself religious?

"Folks whar I'm from all believe on Jesus."

Do you think America is headed in the right direction?

"I believe if we'd not strayed from how it wuz meant to be we'd be in Eden still, loaferin' by the river o' life. 'Stead o' diggin' taters out o' rocks, like muh people do now."

Who do you consider to be your people?

"Appalachian-Americans, o' course."

Why do you want to serve on board the UnderGod?

"I reckon this is the direction America is headed. If yer fer it er agin' it yew might as well precipitate right along with it." The segment ends on that pensive note.

Lark speed-dials Desmond's work number. "Desmond, you're a genius! I don't how you found him, but I love him, this—this—hillbilly art historian. Such twang in his voice. Such hunger in his smile. Hunt him down! Sign him up! The hounds, Desmond! Unleash the hounds! A home phone and a cell, if he has one which is doubtful by the look of him. And do a focus-group. Get the metrics on his authenticity."

What a last minute rush! A bonus high note on which to end a superb week of accomplishment. Now the adrenaline has peaked. It's late and even good little workers must stop sometime, if only so they can work another day. Evor fingers the buttons on his bedside console, causing the light to fade and the sounds of Mozart—lovely, lilting Mozart—fill the room. Evor gives the pillows a final fluff and a tap full of love.

He thinks back to the gobs of hard work that have gotten him where he is today, the sacrifices, the crazy days at Princeton steeping himself in the works of Machiavelli and Segretti, managing various candidates running for positions in student government. Late nights at the lab with a rubber hammer studying voters' stimulus-and-response. His only relaxation coming on the warm afternoons spent at a nearby lake in idle stone-throwing at the windsurfers while his golden retriever McKinley lay in the shade chewing on an old flip-flop.

Evor's mind wanders, drifts, sleeps.

Later, when the Mozart has gone away and there is only his gentle breathing and the curtains' occasional stirring, he will dream: of silvery-skinned dinosaurs come back to life to gnaw at the bark on the tree of evolutionary theory as push-button robins move with hopeful hops along the branches. And of Swedish nightingales in gilded cages held against their will but only for a while, until things get better, under the tangerine glow of a post-historical sun. During the day he is Evor Lark, a blue-eyed wonder, the envy of us all, with just enough peroxide in his wisps of blonde hair to assure us of a vanity safely diverted; at night his are the dreams of madness.

* * * * * *

Walter Pickett is a study in concentration, spindly frame moving deliberately between suitcase and sock drawer. Rain spatters plastic sheeting he'd nailed to the roof only the day before. Reenie had been after him for weeks on that little chore. It was one of the few chores he'd ever done for her.

Reenie and Walter have been together in the two-room cabin for nine years. Under the applicable statutes, as Walter understood it that made them legally bound; and he was prone to refer to Reenie, out of the range of her hearing, as his common-law wife. It was not a term of which she approved.

She was reclining in their comfort chair, watching him pack, telling the news of two neighbor boys in the service overseas. She stopped mid-sentence, to see if he'd notice but he only continued pairing up socks. She stood, remaining silent, striking a characteristic pose: one foot pointed forward while wrapping a slender arm around her back to touch lightly onto the other, like an awkward girl wondering if she could be a ballerina.

"You wuz right," Walter said, straightening up from his packing. "I should've bought new underwears. These 'uns may not git me fur as I need to go."

She went to the kitchen where a pot simmered. Sighing, she stirred it. Her hair done up in the back the way he liked and all he could do was go on about holey underwear.

The suitcase closed with a snap.

"Reenie," Walter called out. "I'm goin' a-voyagin' now."

She was at the table, seated with an unsought-for poignance in front of a single bowl, glancing at him as he shuffled in the doorway weighed down with a suitcase.

She indicated her lonely meal.

"Yew shore yew don't want none?" she said.

"I'm a little fluttery inside."

"Won't seem long," he went on for about the umpteenth time. "Bout a year they tell me. Then I believe things'll be diff'rent. Be a better life. Better'n this."

Now she was standing, arms folded in front as she considered his reasoning.

"It's a fine romance yer offerin'," she said. "Abandonin' me in the bloom of muh youthful beauty to go on yer adventuresome journey."

"Could be a blessin' fer both of us. I wisht yew'd see it that way."

"Enos Slaughter was by t'other day offerin' the loan o' his cow in yer absence. Seemed mighty attentive to muh situation."

"That so. Yew gonna run off with that 'ole pig farmer?"

She turned away.

"He's single an' he works harder'n some I know," she said bravely. "An' after all I ain't married neither."

"Let's not aggervate."

"Sometimes a woman kin improve a man's personal habits. Not always."

"I got to go, Reenie. Yew gonna say good-bye?"

She let him hold her.

She said, "Maybe yew'll git a chance to express all that peculiar deepness yew have inside."

"I'm countin' on yew bein' here upon muh return. Yer the reason I'm doin' this."

She shoved him away with a disbelieving purse of her lips.

"Tut Walter, yer doin' this fer yerself not me and not the Appalachian-American community lak yew been tellin' them reporters. I don't begrudge yew yer opportunity in life. Yew jes got to understand if an opportunity comes along fer me, I got the same right to pursue it."

There was no easy reply to this worrisome bit of reasoning.

"Move to the city," he said at last, trying to make huskiness sound like authority. "With Toby an' his. Wouldn't be near so lonesome."

She gave a laugh that she hoped sounded carefree. "Don't worry 'bout me. I got the lightnin' bugs for company. It'll be grand."

In the barest drizzle after the parting embrace, he took a little fox-trail out of the clearing. It rose to a brambly field, creeping along a low stone wall out to the Skeet Ridge Turnpike where he hitched a ride to the bus station at Justification Junction.

Time to think, on that bumpy Greyhound down the haze-covered mountains. She'd done her hair up the way he liked. He should have said something, been more expressive. Maybe she'd understood without him saying it. Nine years should count for something.

Maybe he should've told her about the phone call from this Evor Lark.

How Lark had said there was to be a mole on board the UnderGod. A mole who'd instigate a mutiny which if successful, would generate for the mole a substantial cash prize. And that he'd agreed to be the mole. She might not have understood; she could be judgmental. Her standards were high about some things.

Being a mole, instigating a mutiny. These weren't things Walter was proud of, but we can't be proud of all our actions. That would be excessive pride, which is a kind of sin, he was pretty sure.

He looked out the window. It was all a little hazy.

* * * * * *

A morning begun in drifting fog and the rhythmic slapping of waves against the pilings. Orange-jacketed men setting up detours with stumbling, sleepy movements. Sharp-eyed birds perch on wire, in expectation. Then a flush from the east routs the mist! And lights the tops of towering spars.

The UnderGod lies anchored at the tip of the Beaufort peninsula. Fishermen dangle feet from the pier, poles extended, their focus-on-fish disrupted by the unprecedented bustle surrounding the handsome old ship.

Tents are raised, grills established. Workmen push and kick a crimson carpet down the asphalt walk leading to the UnderGod's gangway. Battle-hardened employees of Green Zone Security Services provide proprietary assessments into headsets for the benefit of unseen listeners.

In a small park fronting onto the harbor, Evor Lark surveys the scene. He saw that it was good: banners and bunting strewn on poles; vendors in various stages of setting up their booths, carting in frozen patties and packaged buns and tubs of juices and soda. Christian rock bands plugging in speakers and amps, making awful screeching sounds as they adjust their instruments. A retired army major has already set off on an ill-fated attempt to break the record for consecutive squat thrusts (he would be hobbled by a groin pull).

A little after seven Desmond brings to the grateful Evor his first coffee-drink of the morning, a colossus enclosed in styrofoam. Evor cradles it as he thinks. Those complaining men, those fishermen, gone away now, back to where? To buy what? Life was full of fascination.

Eight o'clock is welcomed with a selection of hymns and departure-themed madrigals performed by the doe-eyed Children of Anaheim.

Fronted by a phalanx of microphones and cameras, pastors give their blessings and pose for pictures. Protesters—in limited numbers, valued for the patina of democratic dissent they lend to the proceedings—hold signs decrying the voyage's cost, and its motives. The cameras of the Opticon Network, placed atop ice cream trucks and fit snug into the coils of razor wire marking off the event's perimeter, record everything.

It was good. It was all good.

The Everlasting Gospel marching band, rendering with verve and flair a mélange of fight songs and hip hop favorites sets off on a double-columned high-step down the crimson-coated path, veering with a downward dip to either side as they take up positions near the gangway, still continuing their foot-tapping fusillade. A family dressed in the breech-pants and petticoats of the Puritans comes next, waving in friendship from the pages of history to the curious crowds beginning to form. At Evor's signal, balloons are released, then doves, then tri-colored confetti, then tri-colored doves.

A contingent representing the Veterans of Preventative Wars is next, some wheeled, others walking on the modern-day miracles of prosthetics, acknowledging the increasing applause.

The launch is being co-hosted for the Opticon Network by the once-dashing Stanley Jivens, leading man from long ago on the London stage, chosen for the classy, British quality he lends to the proceedings. Describing the scene for the viewers at home from a second-story café balcony overlooking the main activity, Jivens will serve as a kind of gentleman's host for the Voyage.

"Here come the crew themselves," he is saying on-camera, "ordinary chaps from all walks of life, duffel bags filled with the scant clothing and personal possessions we'll be allowed. Not a man jack of them had sailed a ship three weeks ago but they've been on board the UnderGod all that time getting a crash course in the essentials. Their entrance here is largely ceremonial. I can't stress enough that conditions on board ship will be quite close. Strict limits apply to the size of each crew member's kit. I myself am being forced to leave behind several containers of rather essential grooming products.

"Overhead if we can get a shot—that's it—in flawless military formation it's the Blue Angels, pride of the US Air Force. If you've never seen them perform in person they're really a treat as they swoop down on you, trying to catch you unawares. And of course they're not really angels but the next best thing: fighting men and women in uniform.

"Next marching in smartly is Roland Orr, a bit of a surprise the producers have in store for Luther Dorsey. Roland is a colorful character who had a career as a professional footballer marred by an incident at one of the Super Bowls. He's also acted in the spaghetti westerns, I'm told. Roland and Luther were childhood friends and the fact that Roland was recently arrested on the grounds of one of Luther's eating establishments, and that the Opticon Network has not been shy about publicizing this incident, makes his role on this voyage an intriguing one."

Three young crew members now enter the balcony where Jivens is seated. Two are similar in appearance: fair features, fade-style hair cuts, cotton-flannel shirts and white duck trousers. The third is darker, sullen, with a gold-toothed smile and some dope rope around his neck.

These three have been hand-selected for participation in the Voyage because they combine an edgy, hip-hop energy and a commitment to a centuries-old faith. Evor Lark had insisted: the Voyage had to be hooked up with the urban sub-culture—it wouldn't succeed unless its appeal went beyond the dying demographic that had been Luther's main support in the last election.

Jivens says, "We'll chat now with three young men playing key roles in this grand adventure. Good morning chaps. Have a seat and we'll get acquainted."

Settling into canvas-bottomed director's chairs, they speak in turn to the camera:

"I'm Skip Robbins."

Skip is taller, more commanding than his look-alike Chip.

"I'm Chip Ribbons."

Chip is more youthful and seems vaguely puzzled, like a choir boy trying to read music that is upside down.

"And I'm Rob Dawg, Robbie D. The ultimate OG on the UG. Shout out to Mamma."

"Rob is a product of hip-hop culture," Chip quickly explains.

"But now he's got his Christ on," adds Skip.

"He's a rapper?" asks Jivens.

"Hip-hop artist," corrects Rob. "Goin' hard at all the fake cats."

"Quite," says Jivens. "I want to make sure I have the names. That's Skip Robbins, Chip Ribbons and your last name young man, is Dog? Is that D-o-g?"

"Don't identify myself with a last name," says Rob. "Got one name. Like Diddy. Or Fiddy. You feel me?"

"Ah, no, that couldn't have been me," the puzzled Jivens replies. "It's just I'm a stickler for detail and I'm also host so I want to get things right. Could you spell your last name?"

Rob says, "Yo! Lionel Barrymore! I'm hooked up with G and Imma like to apostleize 'bout that but you keep askin' my last name. Why you act a foo'?"

Skip says, "Rob, remember your anger management."

Chip says, "You give love, you get love, Rob."

Jivens persists.

"Surely on your birth certificate, at the hospital, it said Dog or even D-o-e...."

Rob says, "Dawg is a modifier of my name, of which I have only one. Rob. I do not get mail addressed to Mr. Dawg. Can you articulate with that?"

Jivens makes a hopeful turn to Skip and Chip. "Are you two related?"

"Our last names are different," points out Skip.

"But in a way we are," says Chip. "By our love of Christ."

Skip and Chip high-five.

"Can you explain the role you'll have on board the UnderGod? I must confess I myself don't know the extent of it."

"We'll be Luther's lieutenants," says Skip. "His right-hand men. Though we'll take sailing direction from Captain Braga."

"You and Chip have nautical backgrounds?" says Jivens, glancing at his notes.

"Used to sail our dad's catamarans," says Skip. "Sundays after church."

"We're having abundant lives," says Chip. "Ask us why."

Rob says, "Sundays I used to jack a gank whip in my hood, then we'd strip it and kick down some mary jane 'til the po-po got chill. That was my abundant life."

Arm around Rob, Chip says, "Now he follows Jesus instead of Snoop Dogg."

"I follow both! They both riding for the same cause!"

"My bad," says Chip. They bump fists.

"You've been undergoing rather rigorous training in preparation for this voyage?" Jivens asks, eyes now glued desperately to Skip and Chip.

Skip explains.

"At the New Covenant Naval Academy, we immersed ourselves in 19th-century sailing techniques, even taking the UnderGod on some practice runs. We got as far as Bermuda."

"It's real old school," says Chip.

"We be like ancient mariners," says Rob.

"I'm sure you'll be a formidable triumvirate," says Jivens.

Skip and Chip exchange glances.

"That sounds kind of elitist," Skip objects.

"Is that word even *in* the Bible?" asks Chip.

"Ain't nothin' rhymes with triumvirate," Rob observes. "You use a word like that in normal conversation, shows you got no flow."

"What a shame," Jivens interjects. "I'm being given the signal for passengers and crew to board ship. I'm sure we'll see more of each other in the months to come. Thanks for popping by."

"You're very welcome," says Skip.

"Please accept a pocket-sized edition of the story of Job as a thank you gift," says Chip.

"Peace out," says Rob, who then leans close and whispers to Jivens, "Word up, wanksta. The Dawg still has bite. You wanna bring it, we know how to handle it."

Jivens blanches, and wonders if the beer vendors are pouring yet.

At the foot of the UnderGod gangway, a raven-haired reporter has corralled an animated Blaze Dorsey.

"Blaze, it must be difficult as your husband prepares for this voyage, not knowing when or even if he'll return."

"I fought like a she-devil to be included," says Blaze. "But Luther said a woman on a ship full of men is nothing but trouble. Birds and bees stuff."

The reporter nodded. "The White House this morning issued a statement emphasizing the Voyage of the UnderGod is a private adventure and that while the President is sympathetic and supportive, the US military will not provide assistance. Your reaction?"

"Complete agreement. Our troops are overseas defending our country and that's where they belong. The UnderGod's going to be on its own."

"Blaze, what does Luther hope to accomplish on this voyage?"

Blaze blew a strawberry-peach gum bubble and popped it. Then she gazed at the distant horizon.

"To affirm we're one nation under God. That we can still solve any problem under the right leadership. And maybe lessen our country's dependence on foreign oil by showing these old sailing ships can still get the job done."

"What about potential liabilities? Is it true no insurance company will touch this voyage?"

"Each sailor has signed a pre-nautical agreement we think is iron-clad and consistent with biblical principles. We're also self-insured thanks to donations of as little as five dollars from tens of thousands of Americans."

"The UnderGod has some impressive guns. Is Luther going to use them?"

"Luther's not looking for a fight. But he'll be ready if he finds one."

The final question—"Is this a crusade?"—is drowned by onlookers' shouts as Skip, Chip and Rob Dawg make a startling appearance in the red carpet area, turntable in tow. In dedication to the captain under whose command they would serve, and to the idea of the Voyage itself, the trio would now perform their own original versification, a bit of musical graffiti if you will, a small gesture in the direction of hip hopera: they would rhyme the story of man—from the Creation up until the present moment.

"Kick it," cues Rob Dawg and shouting in unison the trio launches a series of exuberant and highly choreographed movements, punctuated by scratching vinyl:

Rob: "This is how it all began!"
Skip: "Back in the beginnin'?
Rob: "It was Yahweh!"
Chip: "God!"
Rob: "That Who Am Izzle!"
Skip: "Up high!"

Chip: "In the sky!"

Rob: "And that's fo' shizzle!"

Skip: "He was chill."

Chip: "He was real"

Rob: "He was solid bumpin'"

Skip: "But the groove went flat"

Chip: "He said 'I need sumpin!'"

Skip: "So He spoke the Word."

Chip: "Made the sea and the turf."

Skip: "And the creepy, creepin' things."

All: "That! Creep! On Earth!"

Skip: "Made man from the dust."

Chip: "And a woman from a rib."

Rob: "Then God chased man."

All: "Right outta his crib!"

Skip: "God said, 'Adam'

Chip: "'Why you eat from that tree?'"

Skip: "Adam said, 'God'"

Rob: "'Why you hatin' on me?'"

"Holla if you like the way we roll!" Rob Dawg calls out, to knowing nods.

Skip: "God said, 'Man!'"

Chip: "'Get your act together!'"

Rob: "'Or the forecast calls'"

All: "'For some nasty weather!'"

Skip: "But He's a God of love"

Chip: "Yeah! Mercy! Kindness!"

Skip: "We made in his image."

Rob: "That's the tie that binds us!"

Skip: "So He sent his Son!"
Rob: "For our ill behavior!"
Skip: "That's Christ!"
Chip: "JC!"
Rob: "My personal Savior!"

Chip flings himself down now, spinning on his upper back in a whirligig movement known as breaking-in-tongues.

Skip: "Now the end times comin'"
Chip: "And the devil's fixin'"
Skip: "To bust his move"
Rob: "Wid' da six-six-sixin.'"
Skip: "Dead folks!
Chip: "No jokes!"
Rob: "Satan starts cappin'!'"
Skip: "Heathens all"
Chip: "Filled with awe"
Rob: "Wonder what's happenin'"
Skip: "Revelations!"
Chip: "Tribulations!"
Rob: "Got to man the battle stations!"
Skip: "Leader's got to know"
Chip: "'Bout the deali dealio"
Skip: "Who's he gonna be?"
All: "Luther D! Luther D!"
Chip: "Leader's got to know!"
Skip: "'Bout the deali dealio!"
Chip: "Who's he gonna be?"
All: "Luther D! Luther D!"

Thus summoned, Luther himself emerges from a window-tinted, super-sports-luxury-assault-utility vehicle. He is wearing red and blue UnderGod sweatpants and matching top and a white baseball cap tilted and turned to the side that reads "Captain-UG."

The raven-haired reporter leaves Blaze in the lurch and runs to him, demanding with a thrust of her cordless mike, "Talk about this journey you're about to undertake."

Luther looked thoughtful.

"I think of it as more than a journey. It's a voyage of destiny. I feel as if we're being called from beyond the stars."

"There are some, critics if you will, who would criticize you for saying that."

"On what grounds?" said Luther.

"That God doesn't involve himself so closely in human affairs."

"If that were true it would mean I'm hallucinating. Or hearing-impaired. And I'm neither. Just a man with a calling."

"From beyond the stars," said the reporter, still out of breath from her sudden dash.

Luther said, "Now if you'll excuse me, I'm going to answer that call."

Turning to the camera for her sign-off, the reporter said, "Word. That was Luther Dorsey's last statement before embarking on what will be—for him and all you viewers—an incredible adventure."

Luther, holding his breath in a nearby facility, was holding in much more besides: a nameless fear. He'd sounded confident, he knew, almost glib. How much was an act he wasn't sure. He dared not show frailty. Hundreds of crew members and their families were looking to him for leadership. A nation would be watching too, the greatest nation in the world. Help me Lord, he prayed. Help me do Your Will, fulfill Your Plan. I hope this time You mean it.

There was more he wanted to say but no time to say it. Adjusting his sweats, he swung the radiant yellowish-blue door outward and ambled up the gangway in his stiff, reluctant manner. The doe-eyed Children of Anaheim sang, "The World's for Saving."

The UnderGod crew, in military formation, stiffened at Skip Robbins' command. Above them the rigging was taut, the yards square. Cables shone in the sun. Decks were sanded clean. The digital microcameras of the Opticon Network were affixed to the masts and booms and innumerable other locations. Red lights were on. It was go time.

Luther made his first address to the crew. He held a Bible aloft.

"At its founding America was a Christian nation. Favored above all others. Over time our lifestyle became the envy of the world. Our wealth and power were without equal.

"Is it a coincidence this way of life is endangered now just as we've allowed our faith to be diluted into a secular stew of tolerance and magic mood rings? As we attend the Church of Whatever singing faint praises to the deity called I'm-Not-Sure?

"Here is what I believe. God led each of us on board this ship today. To be a part of this moment. He is with us now. He is the source of the faith and courage I see glimmer in your eyes.

"Our time together will not be easy. There will be hard work. Danger and sacrifice. If this does not meet your expectations, if you feel you have been deceived in any way, then there is your means of escape."

He pointed to the gangway. Not a man stirred.

"And so you remain. And thereby give a sacred pledge to obey orders and faithfully execute your duties. Keep this pledge and you will find this voyage to be its own reward.

"Now to a few details of organization. Day-to-day discipline and operation of the ship are entrusted to these three fine, young Christian

Conjuring up the image of a tall ship, the modern mind cannot but imagine wind and sail doing the work, that the crew has ought to do but idle at the rail, eyes peeled for mermaids. The reality is not so fanciful, as the men learned that first day.

Braga had them overhauling the rigging and making frequent adjustments of sail. Skip and Chip divided them into watches and set in place the myriad of details that would govern shipboard routine over the coming months. Rob roved the decks, searching for irregularity. Max Winter offered quiet encouragement, sneaking in quick strokes of his ginger mustache when he thought no one would be the wiser. Luther stayed below.

Before they knew it six bells rang and dinner appeared, hauled up from the galley in large pots. They ate in the open air, seated cross-legged or leaning on the bulwarks or against one of the snub-nosed carronades that populated the upper decks.

First night's menu was salted beef and hard biscuit. It would vary little thereafter. Not a few of the men were made queasy from the rolling motion of the sea, and these could manage only a few mouthfuls. A kitchen hand stood with a ladle, near a barrel with the word "Under-Grog" stenciled on it, but none availed themselves of its contents.

Max Winter moved among them. "This is what they ate back then," he said in response to their grumbles. "You wanted to be sailors. Well now you're sailors."

The meal consumed, they divided into their watches, which would work at four-hour intervals. The first watch manned their posts at eight bells as the others either strolled the decks or went below for a nap. At midnight the first watch roused out the second and took its turn in the hammocks.

They had caught a fair breeze and the yards were trimmed and the studding sails set alow and aloft and the UnderGod sheared off foam as it glided eastward through luminous waters. Chip Ribbons paced his rounds with precision, taking turns at near-right angles, scanning the horizon, aided by the moon's bright glow, stopping now and again to exchange a word with a man being sick at the railing.

And so they left behind the shallow waters above the downward sloping continental shelf to sail out over the deep-sea basins where, in the depths below, there were unseen wonders and treasures and monsters hiding in inky blackness.

* * * * * *

Next morning the men were made to wash the decks, a task to be repeated at the start of each new day. Breakfast consisted of an unidentifiable meat tucked into a tasteless dough and coffee in tin cups. They ate in quiet. At the meal's conclusion a muttering arose among them, led by those from the larger cities, suffering not only from the stomach upset of the first twenty-four hours at sea but also caffeine deprivation.

"You call this coffee?" came a belligerent call.

"What do you mean?" said the ever-present Max Winter.

"It's not coffee! It's swill!"

"I'm not certain but I believe swill's lighter in color," said Max, who drank only peppermint-flavored tea.

"Is there or is there not an espresso machine on board?" they demanded.

"I don't believe so," said Max.

"No steamed milk!" The muttering took on an ugly aspect.

"What about a bean grinder?"

"I can check," said Max but Skip Robbins, nearby, shook his head.

"Remember, nineteenth century," said Skip. "Coffee came in a can."

"But in the name of God at least it could be Starbucks!" cried a man from the Northwest, accustomed to starting his day with cinnamon sprinkles. Skip Robbins shook his head once more, sadly repeating the words, "Product placement."

It was then they noticed the 'Maxwell House' logo on the bottom of their tin cups.

"Not even Folgers!" they cried, flinging the worthless brown liquid onto the deck.

Walter Pickett, seated next to Roland, gave him a nudge. 'You got somethin' to say 'bout this?" Walter said lowly to Roland, who looked surprised and shook his head no. Walter stood and indicated the tub labeled 'UnderGrog', where a bored steward stood in grasp of a ladle.

"How 'bout some o' that corn juice?" Walter said, raising his voice so they all could hear.

Skip looked at Max. The nineteenth-century US Navy had indeed allowed two "tots" of grog per day, one after breakfast and another at dinner.

Walter said, "I heard we wuz strivin' fer historical acc'racy. Those ole-time sailors musta fought like cats fer this stuff."

"You're not *supposed* to drink UnderGrog," said Skip.

"You're *allowed* to," Max explained.

"Well," said Walter with a devilish grin, "whut would Jesus do?"

Stepping to the tub he hefted a ladle, adding as if in apology, "Our Savior lived life to its fullest." Downing his grog in a greedy gulp, he wiped a sleeve onto his flushing face and watering eyes.

"A little dab'll do ya," he pronounced with an audible belch. With Walter's example before them, the men lined up for their portions of UnderGrog and the crisis was averted.

Max Winter said lowly to Skip, "That was a close one. Who's that fellow with the heavy accent?"

"Pickett," whispered Skip. "Walter Pickett."

"Not sure what would have happened if he hadn't stepped in," said Max. "Whose watch is he on?"

"Not exactly on a watch. We've got him down below looking after the livestock. He's some kind of hillbilly so we figured he'd be good with the animals."

"He's one to keep an eye on," said Max.

At mid-morning a shout from the foremast lookout.

"Ship ahoy!"

"Assume shunning positions!" commanded Skip Robbins at once. To avoid any contact with the modern world, in fulfillment of the requirement of historical accuracy, it had been decided the entire crew would turn their backs whenever a modern vessel came within view.

"Begin shunning!" Skip shouted and all backs turned to the offending vessel, in this case an aging tramp steamer, the last of a dying breed.

"Shun them," said Skip in soft incantation, gazing into their turning-away eyes. "Shun them my lovelies. Shun them well. Look to each other. Look to the flag. See it above, proud and free. Here, your allegiance. Here, your duty. Shun them in the morning, shun them in the evening, shun them late at night."

Skip continued talking in this manner, long after the steamer had been lost to view. This ritual would be repeated at each encounter with another vessel. If it happened that ships were simultaneously seen in opposing directions then the men were made to flatten themselves on the decks and gaze up at the uncontaminated sky as the officers paced among them, reciting the soft song of refusal.

A few uneventful days, then the clouds ahead condensed, the seas grew choppy. The UnderGod heaved and pitched among the waves. Birds appeared in thick flocks; porpoises swam swiftly by on unknown errands. They had encountered the powerful Gulf Stream. The turbulence was the result of this north-flowing current meeting the eastward winds pushing them forward.

Once the seas grew calm they saw floating clumps of a thick, greenish-brown grass. Braga called it gulfweed and pronounced they had arrived at the edge of the Sargasso Sea, the enormous, oval-shaped area stretching half the length of the south Atlantic.

Bordered by surging currents, the Sargasso remains undisturbed by them: its skies are clear, its waters warm and heavy with salt and gulf-weed. Its inhabitants are mostly small, luckless animals swept by the currents from their original coastal habitats and deposited in the ocean's middle, forced to survive on a grassy island, holding fast to branching fronds lest they drop off into the abyss.

On the UnderGod the general mood was enthusiasm. The crew was pulling together, engaging in spirited competition to see who could be first to mount a mast or tie a sturdy knot. Luther appeared on deck in these early days, conferring with Braga, working with his shirt off where the cameras could catch sight of him, side-by-side with his crew in the midday sun.

But as the days passed Luther could more often be found below deck studying scripture, talking on the videophone to Evor Lark, even writing the occasional letter to Blaze. Day-to-day operations were left to Braga and the trio of lieutenants, with Max as Luther's cat's paw. When a dispute did rise to Luther's level he tended to resolve it in favor of the men, saying he saw no point in working them to death this early in the voyage.

Luther's first encounter with Roland was awkward. At a glance they took each other in, mutually appalled at what the other had become. Roland found most leaders lacking; Luther was no exception. He saw in Luther's face the petty moralism that had plagued him his whole life. We make our own gods, Roland believed, and what an ugly God Luther had fashioned for himself, one lacking in humor or justice.

In Roland's constant joking and play-acting Luther saw a pathetic clinging to youth in an attempt to evade life's serious questions. He'd always thought Roland lacking in humility and piety and he suspected any misfortunes Roland had suffered in life were from his own making.

On a long voyage an initial excitement in the early stages is often followed by a mental slump. The sea, overwhelming in its size and mystery, possesses great monotony, each day passing like the one before. No house, no tree, no snowy peak lend interest to the scenery. No songbird lifts its voice at dawn. The routine can be broken by a squall, the sight of land, a sail with news from home. But for the UnderGod in the middle of the Atlantic there was no land and the weather was mild and when they saw another ship they shunned it.

The top men's scampers grew less energetic; the daily scraping and cleaning more wearisome. Luther's despondency returned; he was second-guessing himself on the entire venture. Evor Lark provided positive reports on the ratings and how pleased the advertisers were but at the same time said we can do better, and he pushed for Luther to be on camera more.

You're the star, Evor said. Audiences need to see you on deck, giving commands, receiving reports, eyeing the distant horizon. (And what about Walter Pickett, said Evor. Who? said Luther. Walter Pickett, he seems very authentic, said Evor. Ask Max about him.)

It's difficult to maintain a confident front when inside you feel hollow and fraudulent. In the dungeon of his mind, where his hope was sometimes kept in manacles, Luther feared it could happen again, on board this ship: rejection. The crew, the voters, the people—call them what you will—could turn on him without warning. God could play His tricks.

He sometimes found himself thinking of Blaze. Her quirky ways, her constant exercising, her mannerisms, he felt certain some of them must have been endearing. He felt more tenderness for her in her absence than he'd ever felt in her presence.

Even Max Winter, less given to emotional swings, felt a certain sag. There were friends to miss, games of whist, the side yard garden where he spent Sunday mornings after service. He'd brought books on board but now had regrets about those left behind. Most of all he worried about Luther. Max could see the haunting shadows returning to his leader's face, but didn't know how to make them go away.

Roland had the least to miss. The sea and its ever-expanding horizon suited him. The tumbleweed is happy wherever it is blown. The discipline though, the dreary chores, these he could not abide.

Each Sunday in the early afternoon the men assembled in formation on the main deck for review in their cleanest, brightest outfits and Luther strode among them—arms folded, inspecting,—asking questions such as what town were they from, and did they miss their sweetheart.

Standing before Roland one day as the deck rolled gently beneath them, Luther ignored an irregular knot and instead laughed and clapped Roland on the shoulder because Roland was wearing a tee shirt that said, "Born to Scrub."

"Born to scrub," said Luther. "That's the spirit. That's the attitude, men. Accept your responsibilities. Embrace them. Excellent spirit, Roland, excellent."

Luther continued his review as the men remained at attention. Walter Pickett eyed Roland thoughtfully.

The next morning the main hatchway lifted up and a snare drum beat a rolling, shuffling rhythm and Rob Dawg blew a silver whistle, yelling down into the forecastle: "Yo! All hands at stations! All hands on deck! Man the station! Jump up!"

Thus was announced the first of many such drills—dress rehearsals in the event of a foreign vessel initiating hostilities against the white-sailed UnderGod.

The men scrambled to the gun decks and the various cannons and engaged themselves in tasks of ramming and sponging. Soon covered in powder and sweat, they loaded and fired, sending lead and old iron out across an unappreciative ocean. Others fetched water or pretended to carry the dead and wounded below or relayed messages from one part of the ostensibly smoke-covered ship to another. Luther shouted commands from an observation post on the quarter deck platform.

When the guns had been given a good firing, a shift in pretension was announced with a cry of, "Drill to repel boarders!"

The unseen enemy was now said to be swarming alongside in small boats, attempting to board with the aid of grappling hooks and the UnderGod's own ladders.

Weaponry was issued: pikes for poking, pistols to blow out brains, short-handled dirks for the tactic of jab and thrust. Engaging in this shadow warfare in a compliant and dutiful manner, the men were obedient to command but aware of a certain ridiculousness in the proceedings. The drills made them conscious again of the almost-forgotten cameras.

Roland, in his characteristic way, went above and beyond the spirit of the activity, whirling about in a celebration of human movement: a dancer pirouetting among windmills, a matador in a ring surrounded by bulls, a knight defending the honor of a beleaguered queen. He envisioned attackers leaping from the shrouds, crawling out of the small boats, tip-toeing in along the bow-sprit like malignant cats.

He thrust his sword so often and with such gruesome result he proclaimed it soggy with the blood of the imaginary enemy and demanded another. The officers of the UnderGod, at first pleased with such high energy, soon perceived a not too-subtle mockery.

Hailing the Canary Islands, the men were given a half-day shore leave. Roland returned in good spirits, parrot perched on a shoulder.

He named the bird the Ministry of Information since he'd obtained it in an open air market across from a building of that same name. The Ministry of Information had feathers of a velvety pea-green color and a head crowned in cherry-red and he spent his days caged on a shelf near Roland's hammock, squawking and listening and pecking at the crumbs of hardtack the men threw his way.

A series of conversations took place between Luther and Max on the subject of Roland. "Make him part of the ownership society," Max argued. "Put him in situations of responsibility. Make him feel this is his voyage too."

Luther said he was worried about the appearance of favoritism, but allowed himself to be persuaded. It was decided Roland should take a turn as officer-in-charge of a night watch, while the ship still enjoyed the mild weather of the lower latitudes.

The night of Roland's command came calm, a bright moon reflecting in a shimmering line along the surface of the sea up to the Under-God's oaken hull. Sensing Roland's permissiveness, most of the watch found a place for sleep—a carronade-slide, the shelter of a weather rail. Roland tucked himself away under a tarp in one of the small boats. There was no one to notice the band of armed men who appeared suddenly on board, as if dropped from the sky.

"There is no God but God," the intruders murmured, creeping among the sleeping crew.

"Allahu Akbar!" they whispered in exaltation, placing daggers against the throats of each silently awakened man.

As the intruders rounded up the last of the watch, the alarm was sounded. The crew of the UnderGod rushed on deck and a standoff ensued, the outnumbered intruders keeping the crew at bay with threats made about their hostages.

"Careful," warned Max Winter in his night shirt. "Life means nothing to them."

Luther, roused from his cabin, went immediately to the forefront.

"Let my men go," he commanded.

"Not until Saddam is returned to power," hissed an intruder, tip of a blade touching a hostage's neck.

"We hate your freedoms!" asserted another dutifully.

"Renounce your God, Luther Dorsey," cried a third. "Or we will kill these hostages. Starting with this simple grocer from a small town."

Roland, emerging from his small boat hideaway, watched the proceedings with an unalarmed interest. He whispered to a man next to him, "What's a grocer?"

"You know, he works in a supermarket."

"The guy that swipes your stuff at the register? He's a checker."

"What about the guy who puts the food in the bags?"

"He's a bagger," said Roland.

"The one behind the meat counter?"

"If anything, a butcher," said Roland.

"Then who's the grocer?"

"That's what I'm asking."

A glare from Rob Dawg silenced the idle speculation.

"So that is my choice," Luther was saying loudly. "Renounce my Savior or innocent lives are given over to terrorists. What negligence has led to this unspeakable dilemma?"

"Your watchmen were asleep!" guffawed an intruder. Luther's eyes sought out Roland.

"Suppose I offered my own life in place of theirs?" Luther said. "Take me as your hostage. For I am ultimately responsible for what happens on board this ship."

The pirates, conferring among themselves, became argumentative, gesturing with their hands and hooks, staking out seemingly irreconcilable positions. The crew saw their chance. Surging forward as one, they overpowered the distracted brigands, who seemed caught completely off guard and failed to harm a single hostage.

"Well done men," said Luther.

To the captured pirates he said, "You may take off your disguises."

Bandanas and eye patches were removed and black markings wiped away; the invaders revealed themselves to be Skip, Chip, Rob and a few other recognizable faces.

Luther spoke so they all could hear. "This wasn't a real attack. If it had been, we might all be dead. As a group, we performed well, although certain among us were lax. We never know when the enemy will strike or what awful weapons he will bring to the battle. Let's turn in. Tomorrow we work for improvement."

The pirate attack was promoted by the Opticon Network as Operation Eternal Vigilance, complete with its own theme song and crossed-swords logo. As with so many other issues of the day, viewer reaction was synchronized to political leaning. A left-wing blogger labeled it a fake and a farce and a disgrace to "whatever it was supposed to be."

The right saw sacrifice and heroism, best summed up by the editors of the *Wall Street Journal*:

> "... *however real or staged you think the attack was (and we, for our part, will wait until the facts are all in before judging), seeing Luther Dorsey's courageous performance on that bright and perilous night, this much has to be clear: there isn't a woman in America right now who wouldn't want to bear his children.*"

Blaze, in a Voyage-centered blog of her own, fired off this friendly rejoinder: "Back off ladies, I'm first in line for that assignment."

The UnderGod fell in with a fair breeze, its topgallant studding-sails spread high above and the flag trailing behind from the mizzenmast in fearless innocence. At the weekly review, those who had led the recapture of the ship were called forward so Max Winter could pin medals to their chests, commemorating their bravery in battle. Luther observed the proceedings. Walter Pickett was among the recipients.

"Keep up the good work," said Max.

"Fer the greater glory," said Walter.

Roland's tee shirt read 'Paper or Plastic?'

"I don't get that," Luther said to Max as the men dispersed. "Do you get that, paper or plastic?"

"Not exactly," said Max. "Post-modern irony, I suppose. That may be the whole point—that 'squares' like us don't get it."

"He's mocking us," said Luther. "Is that it? He's mocking all that we stand for."

Roland, mending a sock later that day in the shade of a bulwark, was approached by one of Luther's cabin boys.

"He wants to see you," said the youth.

Roland found Luther at his writing desk, deep in thought.

"Have a seat, please," said Luther, reaching to flick a wall-switch. "There. That turns off the camera. Gives us a chance to speak man to man. I know we haven't had much time for getting reacquainted. A lot to do on a project like this. How're things working out for you?"

"To be honest Luther, I've had more fun at a Mormon picnic. Cleaning those decks—which you know are really just outdoor floors, I think we lose sight of that—is not my idea of a good time."

"I understand, I understand. But it's what they did in the old days, so what can we do?"

"Luther, you got anything to drink in here? I heard you do."

"As a matter of fact, yes. Want some? Why not? We're old friends."

Luther dug a bottle out from a desk drawer and filled two glasses, which they clinked together and drained like they'd done it all their lives. Luther poured again.

"You know, Myerson owns his own company now," said Roland. "Some kind of specialized software. Three hundred fifty employees. I never would have thought that would happen. That surprises me as much as what you've done."

"You're surprised by what I've done?" said Luther.

"I didn't have you pegged for presidential candidate when we were bird-dogging girls at the mall."

"I don't suppose I looked like I'd amount to much. But then, who does? For some reason, the Lord asked me to do His work."

"You get an invitation? Or you have to apply for the job?"

Luther said, "You haven't changed. You're clever. But you hide behind it. You're hidden away, even from yourself."

"Sounds like I'm going to get counseled."

"I've counseled lots of people. Many say I've helped them turn their lives around."

"I've been headed in the wrong direction too long to turn around now."

"It's never too late. God's heart is always open."

"So's Seven-Eleven. But I don't go to church there."

Luther studied him, unflinching.

"Roland, do you believe in this voyage?"

"You mean like is it real or a dream?"

"I mean why did you agree to participate?"

Roland considered. "It sounded like an adventure and I'm kind of running out of those types of opportunities these days."

Luther continued to study him. "Was that it?"

Roland gave his mischievous grin. "To be honest, I didn't have anything much better to do. That was probably the main reason."

Luther tried another approach. "What matters to you? What's important? Is there anything you love, apart from yourself?"

Roland thought again. "Football. But that's over. So apart from that…maybe not. Maybe there's nothing I love other than myself. Does that make me a bad person? I don't hurt anyone."

"It means you don't know your true self. You don't realize the purpose for which you were made."

Roland said, "Nobody was made for just one purpose."

Luther said, "Everyone was made for just one purpose. To love the Lord."

Roland said, "Luther, is there anything in particular you wanted to see me about other than the fate of my immortal soul?"

"Yes. I need to know if you're with me or against me. If I can count on you."

"Is that all? Don't worry, I won't mess up your program. That's not why I came."

Luther said, "What about these, ah, tee shirts you've been wearing? What are they supposed to mean?"

"Freedom of expression," said Roland. "It's a very American thing to do."

"Of course. But there's something about them. Something subversive, don't deny it. I can't ban them, that would be too heavy-handed. I won't be drawn into that trap. But I'm asking, as a personal favor, if you'd tone them down."

"Are you ordering me to?"

"I said I don't want to do that. And another thing, the other night. Sleeping on duty. It's inexcusable."

"You mean during the fake pirate attack."

"It was a security drill."

"So if I'd been awake I could have prevented a fake pirate invasion by members of our own crew. I don't understand in the first place why we're working four-hour shifts. I still haven't adjusted to that and I know a lot of the men haven't. That's one of the reasons we sleep so much on our watch."

"What are the other reasons?"

"That there's nothing to do up there except play sentry and tell each other the story of our lives, which I've done three times over with each man on my watch already."

Luther said, "We're being historically accurate. We're proving a point."

"What's the point?"

Luther brought his fist down on the desk, causing their glasses to bounce. "That we're as tough and filled with faith as we've ever been!"

Roland said, "Maybe we could take that for granted and move on."

"Roland, I won't argue with you. Security is paramount. Before we left I learned of chatter among the terrorists about the possibility of a disruptive activity. It could be aimed at us."

"Max go under cover?"

"You're forgetting I was a presidential candidate," said Luther, leaning back. "I still have sources inside the government. People who were hoping I'd win."

Roland finished his drink.

Luther said, "Roland, consider this a warning. Any further lapses will result in disciplinary measures."

"Maybe I should just leave the ship."

"No one leaves the ship until we circle the globe and return to Beaufort Island," said Luther. "You can count on that."

"I'll bet it says that in the contract."

"As a matter of fact it does. You're the master of your fate on this voyage, Roland. It's up to you.

"You may leave now," Luther added, putting his reading glasses back on.

"Aye aye cap'n," said Roland, starting for the door. "One more thing. These Sunday services, seeing as how I'm godless, wouldn't it be better if I didn't attend?"

Luther looked at him over the rim of his glasses. "It will be best, Roland, if you obey the laws of the ship."

"Aye aye cap'n," said Roland, saluting smartly.

IV

THE UNDERGOD LAY BECALMED, unable to fall in with the slightest stirring of air. Braga, taking measurements with his sextant, said in a worried tone, "Here, this is the zero, the area of *saudade*, I forget your word for it."

"The doldrums, you mean?" said Max, as usual observing Braga's activities with interest.

"Yes," said Braga. "Doldrums I think. The air is sleeping. Nothing moves. It may be days before we break free."

The absence of progress did endure and the lack of movement forced the officers to devise new tasks for the crew to perform. The ship was scraped inside and out. The standing rigging coated with tar, the topmast rigging rattled. New seizings and coverings fitted. The capstan and bells, made of brass, were polished bright.

A week of trying and waiting; still the ship remained in place. Another round of innovation in the chores. Hammocks were hand-scrubbed, and hoisted aloft to dry. Swabbing the decks with mops would no longer do. They could better be cleaned, it was determined, with a holystone, soft and flat like pumice with long ropes at each end, allowing it to be pushed and pulled across the deck's open areas. For the corners near the masts and guns, smaller stones were used that forced the men to their hands and knees.

All the while, the heat knew no bounds—the malevolent sun attacking in plain view, knowing no retribution was possible. Brief, drenching squalls provided brief, drenching relief. Then the sun made its inevitable return, oppressing them, withering all impulses of strength and energy. The sea remained still, without a ripple, without a wrinkle.

The air in the forecastle grew stale, dampened from the watery overflow of the various scrubbing operations taking place on the deck above. Hammocks were transformed into swampy repositories for pools of sweat, in which the men tossed and turned for their four-hour period of rest. Then it was a sleepless stagger back up top to take their turn at the watch.

The general level of irritation rose: complaints about the food, squabbles over a supposed remark, a personal slight, real or imagined. The officers observed small groups speaking in lowered voices. Once-innocent gestures now came under suspicion. The officers noticed, or thought they did, the exchange of conspiring glances.

Luther asked for ideas to boost the men's morale. Skip Robbins proposed a competition to calculate how many jelly beans the ship could hold at maximum capacity. Chip Ribbons suggested pop quizzes on the New Testament, with tiny halos awarded for a correct answer. Rob Dawg thought a keelhauling might lift spirits. Braga insisted a ship full of prostitutes could be delivered, without specifying how or by whom ("Your country is so rich! You could easily afford it!"). Luther, his mind absorbing the torpor of the weather that enveloped them, vetoed them all. Nothing was done.

One dismal afternoon Max Winter paid a visit to the lower deck area where Walter Pickett toiled: a dark, cramped world where makeshift pens had been constructed and strewn with straw for the chickens and pigs that provided fresh meat during the long voyage.

"We've certainly got you tucked away down here," said Max, giving an uncertain pet to an equally uncertain pig.

"Yessir. Sometimes I git afeared the trip'll end afore I kin make a positive contribution."

"Maybe we can get you up on top, working the sails. How would you like that?"

"Thank yew kindly, but I'm afeared o' high places. Since yew brung up the subject though, I did have an ideer I'd lak to perpose."

"Certainly Walter. What is it?"

"Sir, in seemin' contrast to muh backwoods manner an' speech, I've been educated in a variety o' scholarly disciplines, the most prominent bein' art history with a emphasis in the later Renaissance o' northern Italy. P'rhaps with yer permission I could present some lectures to the men, which might prove divertin' durin' this time o' tedium and would at the least be upliftin' and educational. I don't see a down side."

"Walter, I had no idea."

"It's all here on my resume, sir. You can keep that, it's a copy."

"Very impressive. You should have spoken up sooner."

"I'm not one to spread muh own feathers."

"What would you use for materials?"

"I brung my own books an' prints, hopin' this opportunity would manifest itself."

"You have my word on it, Walter. I'll arrange it so your first class can be held tomorrow."

Walter said, "Thank yew kindly. I'd shorely enjoy bein' up on deck, elewcidatin' the subtle shadin' of a Tintoretto as opposed to sloppin' hogs down here in the dark.

"No offense fellers," he added, with a glance down at the pigs, who only snorted in response.

The audience for Walter's lecture numbered but a half dozen; even for a bored crew, art history taught by a hog-slopping hillbilly was not a big draw. Roland was among the inquisitive handful that seated themselves in the scant shade offered by the mainmast at midday.

Walter gave an introductory overview, then handed out color reproductions of Portobello's epic triptych, "The March of Vanity."

Walter said, "Portobello is here depictin' a triumphal procession that wuz a common way fer a emperor o' Rome to display the treasure piled up in the process o' bestowin' civilization onto the fringes o' the empire.

"Note how the patrician's banner unfurls with calkilated elegance. An' here the upward movement o' the elongated trumpets is gittin' powerful reinforcement from the vertical spear held in a soldier's hand. An' jes look with what infant joy this young'un peers at his mother's breasts."

A few men snickered. Max, auditing from the back row, frowned.

Walter continued. "The chalice held in this bearer's hands is so big it purt near knocks him over. Portobello goes outta his way to illustrate the empire's power an' reach by emphasizin' the booty it has managed to—"

More snickers at 'booty'.

"—acquire fer itself."

"We turn now to Portobello's Madonnas, marked by their statuesque beauty, in contrast to his naturalistic landscapes, providin' additional evidence—as if it were needed—"

Walter's eyes narrowed and he stopped.

He said, "Fellers I will ask that durin' this lecture we keep all prurient n' juvenile ideers to ourselves an' that applies with specificity to the use o' the word 'hooters', which I find gen'rally inappropriate an' especially so in reference to the masterworks under our consideration.

"Perhaps this is a good stoppin' point. We'll pick up at our next session with Andrea del Sarto's Pieta, whose juxtaposition o' tranquil beauty with a vague sense o' unrest will provide us with a link to the Mannerists to follow. Be shore to tell your shipmates if yew think they'd lak to share in this learnin' experience."

Max approached Walter as the group dispersed.

"I couldn't help thinking, as you were speaking," Max began, "that the Italians can be so sensual. It provides a temptation to the men. If I could suggest updating to someone more spiritual, a modernist I think will rank with the masters when history has had time to collect its thoughts. I'm speaking of Thomas Kinkade."

Walter started as if jolted by an electric eel. He said, "The Master o' Light. His work is purt near unforgivable—forgettable. Unforgettable I meant to say."

"Good. I was afraid you might think him too accessible," said Max. "I know how you specialists can be."

"Art for the masses is muh motto. But it's a dang shame, as I reflect on it, I don't believe I brung with me any samplin's o' his, though I kin double-check."

"Would you? Kinkade would offer fewer distractions. After all, though they're the salt of the earth, our fellow sailors aren't scholars, are they?"

"Ever bit of whut you say is true, Mr. Winter."

Roland too had remained behind, still sitting cross-legged, studying one of the Portobello prints.

"I see you're a thinkin' man's sailor," said Walter, with a glance to ensure Max was out of range. "Allow me to point out some details I elected not to pursue in front of a less exclusive audience. Here fer instance, a woman shouts insults at the emperor, and here this man's fingers fleck the underside o' his chin in a gesture of disrespeck you an' I kin both git the gist of, centuries after the fact. Note how Portobello has provided the emperor with eyes that cross slightly, as if his mental equipment weren't up to snuff."

Roland smiled and said, "You have an interesting eye for detail."

Walter said, "Hidden within Portobello's decorative genius is the incipient beginnin's o' usin' art to undermine the established political order."

"You really think art can do that?"

"Art kin set the table. Takes somethin' extry to serve the main course."

Walter held out his hand and they shook.

Walter said, "Lookin' forward to our next time together."

Luther was in his cabin, seated before the immense communications control panel, talking with Evor Lark via the videophone.

Lark said, "Let's talk ratings. Overseas we're holding up well. Domestically we've fallen off since the pirate attack, but the product spin-offs are going gangbusters. I'm told UnderGrog is the new carrot juice.

"Too bad about these darn doldrums though, can't shake 'em, can we? We need to get to Rio, things will really open up then. We've got undercover cameramen ready to go and native guides to show the crew around town, if you know what I mean."

"I'm not sure I do," said Luther.

"Girls, Luther, girls. Hootchie-kootchie. What do they say these days? Gettin' busy."

Luther said, "Let's put our cards on the table. Do you mean to say you're going to facilitate my men into fornication?"

"They've been at sea for months. I would think their levees are ready to burst by now, don't you?"

"I'm not liking what I hear, Evor."

"Don't worry. We'll snip and clip to stay sensitive to family values. But we need a younger demographic."

"Evor, I will remind you the UnderGod is to be an example, a shining city on a hill. Have you forgotten already those talks we had? Or were you not sincere?"

Evor said, "You can't be an example if no one's watching. Look, with any luck someone gets a venereal disease. Then you have sin, repentance, forgiveness, redemption and gosh, I don't know what else. That's your department."

"I will not expose my men to venereal disease for the sake of the ratings. I'm the ship's captain. The men will get leave only on my approval."

"Luther, I repeat, the ratings are down. You know as well as I do you can't use a flop TV show as a springboard to anything."

"I want to talk to Saul."

"Saul's not around much these days. He's golfing in Scotland. We think he's looking at retiring. He's pretty much told me I'm in charge of this project."

"Back there, maybe. Not out here."

Evor said, "I can see I've roused your inner patriarch. Let's talk in a few days."

At the second of Walter's lectures the audience had shrunk to three: Roland, Max, and a seasick sociologist from San Diego. The subject was the Mannerists of the sixteenth century.

Near the end of the session Walter said, "An artist lak Pontormo had nowhere to run, nowhere to hide from the perfection o' his classical predecessors. So he engaged in a elegant distortion, as if to mock the very ideals classicism had fought to uphold.

"The result wuz a decadent beauty all its own. Note in this here Deposition by Pontormo, there's rilly no effort made to place the characters in a natural landscape. A little fluffy cloud floatin' on its lonesome in the left hand corner—that ain't landscape. An' while the ostensible settin' is an outdoor one, ask yerself: is there a single source o' light? Yew will find there is not. The artist has done away with the sun an' is employin' his own sense o' whar light should be an' whut it should do. Thus did the Mannerists subvert the dominant paradigm with which they wuz confronted. Yes, Dr. Winter?"

Max said, "Couldn't such deviations from God's orderly creation be considered examples of moral flabbiness?"

"Thass a insightful question Dr. Winter, an' I hope I haven't given the impression of a definitive assessment o' these here Mannerists, who in the eyes of a great many critics knew as much about paintin' as a possum does 'bout Puccini. I'll explore this controversy in greater detail at muh next lecture, which I hope yew'll all attend. Class is dismissed."

As Walter gathered his books and prints, Max approached.

"Another enjoyable class," Max said. "Will we be getting to Kinkade soon?"

"Believe we will," said Walter. "I'm jes tryin' to maintain chronological integrity."

"Keep up the good work," Max said. "It's not going unnoticed."

Roland was pawing through Walter's collection of prints, idly rifling through centuries of Europe's greatest artwork. He said, "I noticed Max giving you advice on how to teach the class."

Walter said, "I do believe, lak the song says, everbody's beautiful in their own way. But for whut Thomas Kinkade drips onto a canvas, he should be clapped in irons."

"I'm sure Max means well," said Roland. "We're all God's children."

"Didn't have yew figgered fer a believer," said Walter.

"I'm not," said Roland. "It's just an expression."

That Sunday the afternoon air was sticky and still. Waves lapped list-lessly at the UnderGod's hull. At the weekly review, Luther paced in front, head down, thinking. Roland stood in the front row, quietly at attention, hands folded behind him. His tee shirt said, "I Don't Like Mondays".

Luther stopped in front of him.

"I guess every day seems like Monday, doesn't it?" he said in a boom-ing voice. "It's hard work being a sailor. You're finding that out. I know you're all anxious to get moving again and on to Rio de Janeiro. Our one scheduled stop on the eastern coast of South America. But let's not put all our eggs in one basket. On a long voyage like this, we have to be flexible.

"We're all a little frustrated by the lack of wind, the lack of progress. But I would say this to you: it's a sign God has taken notice of our ad-venture. He has a purpose in creating these meteorological conditions, which Captain Braga assures me are quite extraordinary. Only time and prayer will reveal to us the nature of His purpose."

That evening the three young lieutenants and Max had their customary dinner in Luther's cabin. Luther was somber.

"Gentlemen, I feel within me a profound disturbance. Concerning this voyage, this ship, and these souls we have charge of. Braga confirms we're no closer to South America now than ten days ago. I have con-cluded, after prayerful consideration, that in some unknown manner we have given offense to the Almighty.

"I'd like to see if we can figure out the specifics. Then take corrective action and get this voyage back on track. So the question I put to you is this: what's going down on board the UnderGod? Level with me."

"These fellows would be in the best position to know," said Max, with a nod to the lieutenants. "They work more closely with the crew than I do."

"There's sin on board," said Skip. "For reals."

"We're all sinners," Chip agreed.

"Every last, miserable busta on board," said Rob Dawg.

"The men gamble," said Skip. "Craps, poker."

"Paper, rocks, scissors," Chip added.

"They shirk their duty."

"Tell dirty jokes."

"Sing off-color songs."

"The grog casks have been tampered with."

"They don't pay attention during Bible study sessions."

"I'm not getting' nobody to Saturday morning hip-hop Psalm readings," said Rob Dawg in a subdued tone.

"It's worse than I imagined!" Luther exclaimed. "Why wasn't I told before?"

"It's my fault Luther," said Max. "I'd heard some of this in bits and pieces but I guess I didn't want to burden you with it. You have so much on your mind."

"What's Roland's role?" Luther asked. "The men look up to him, don't they?"

Skip said, "He doesn't take anything seriously. Always has a joke, making fun of the rules. You might say he's a part of whatever's gone wrong."

Chip said, "He was wearing a tee shirt the other day that said, 'Everybody is Everything.'"

"That's just gobblety-gook," said Skip.

"Wiggety-wack," agreed Rob Dawg.

"Crazy cuckoo talk," Chip affirmed.

"All right, enough silliness!" Luther said. "I've decided on a course of action. Max, I want a general assembly in the morning. Special inspection. Make up a reason. Keep them on deck as long as you can. Meanwhile, Skip, Chip, Robbie D., I want every cabin and duffel bag searched. I mean upside down and inside out. Report back after dinner."

"Yes sir!" said Skip with a crisp salute. "What are we looking for, sir?"

"Evil," said Luther. "All the evil you can find. It's here, I feel it. It's angering our Lord and impeding our progress. Your job is to hunt it down."

Chip said, "Sir, won't the men object to having their things searched?"

Luther said, "Not if they have nothing to hide. Besides, it's in the contract."

The next morning the extended inspection was held. The men were made to stand at attention in the hot sun exposed to more than two hours of Max's delaying tactics.

Afterward, Walter Pickett spotted Roland going aloft, the Ministry of Information perched on Roland's shoulder. Walter waited an innocent interval, then climbed up after. As he eased himself over the lip of the crow's nest he gave a bit of a startle to Roland, who'd just used a straw to ingest a small quantity of opium. The floor of the crow's nest was one of the few places Roland could indulge his habit out of the cameras' view. Walter pretended not to notice.

They lay on their backs, using rolled-up sails for cushions, staring at the cloudless sky. The parrot groomed himself.

Walter said, "I've been wantin' to ask 'bout somethin.' If yew find me invasive, I'll keep to my own tomater patch."

"Fire when ready," Roland grunted.

"Whut was it happened that night 'afore the Super Bowl agin' them Cowboys? Yew wuz poised to have a big game. Then yew didn't play a lick. There never wuz no explanation given."

Roland shrugged—the same shrug he always gave when he told this story. "Night before the game I was all keyed up. Couldn't sleep. So I slipped out after they did the bed check, figuring I'd get a quick drink at the bar in the lobby, thought it might calm me down. But the place was packed with fans, everybody recognized me, wanted to shake my hand, buy me another drink. Next thing I know I'm in a private suite in some-body's hot tub. Assistant coach caught me sneaking back into my room at about 4:30, turned me in. Little prick. They deactivated me. Didn't even dress for the game."

"Denied yerself a grab at the glory."

"Yeah."

"Shied away, on the brink o' greatness."

"I think you've got the concept," said Roland.

"Believe yew'll have a chance at redemption on board this ship."

"Why you say that?"

"Jes a feelin'," said Walter. "'Bout Luther's behavior an' how things is developin'."

At this moment a breeze arose. A startling breeze. A breeze of deliv-erance. The sails fluttered to life, enlarging in a sustained way they hadn't in nearly a fortnight. The previously empty skies were suddenly awash in whiteness as a fleece of clouds moved in, overlapping each other, vying for attention.

There was a loud commotion on the deck below. The crew could be observed scurrying to and fro. Braga was directing the top men to lay aloft to set sail. They were leaving the doldrums. The UnderGod was moving again, pointed for South America, leaving twin white trails in her wake.

Roland and Walter, after standing to peer down and take in the sud-denly-busy world below, resumed their rest in the same prone, upward-gazing positions.

Walter said, "When I wuz little I used to picture all manner o' gods an' heavenly creatures hidden amongst the puffs and swirls of a cloudy sky. Spectatin' over our activities."

Roland said, "I guess I figured God or Santa Claus was up there somewhere. I used to get 'em mixed up."

"Santa's from a 'ole Norse myth," said Walter. "Muh daddy taught at the schoolhouse, n' he allus had me to studyin' on the classics so I knew muh religions and mythologies real good. Yew ever study on the classics?"

"A little bit. The one about the big war."

"That would be the Iliad," said Walter at once. "Paris, Achilles, Helen o' Troy."

"Didn't care for Achilles. He was cold. He was a killer."

"Now that produces startlement within me," said Walter. "Man who rose to the ranks o' perfessional football, acted in the motion pictures, had relations with many elegant senoritas—my goodness, yew is Achilles hisself. A hero larger than life."

Roland said, "I've always seen myself as more of an underdog."

"That don't sound too promisin'. Specially when yer dealin' with a overdog like Luther."

Walter rose up again, to stretch and peer down at the bright-work about the great guns and the marvelous whiteness of the decks.

"Ship's not really so hard to figger, is it?" said Walter.

"Never tried to."

"Fellers is fellers," Walter went on matter-of-factly. "Want to know whut to do. Want to know whoever's in charge knows his business."

No response.

"You an' Luther go way back."

"Oh yeah," said Roland. "We wrestled, played ball, hockey when the ponds froze over. Used branches for sticks. Luther'd always get one big as a club and he'd high-stick you with it. Don't let him tell you he didn't."

"Sounds mighty sentimental. But nowadays he don't hardly acknowledge yew on those rarified occasions when he struts about on deck."

"He's got a lot to think about. Big responsibilities."

"This scrubbin' and warshin' they got us goin' on with? Thass a whole lot of little responsibilities, yew ask me."

"Just a drill," said Roland. "There's always a drill. Wherever you go."

"How 'bout searchin' through our private possessions while we's standin' in the hot sun an' that creepy 'ole fool Max Winter examines ever button on our britches? That jes a drill too?"

Roland said, "Nothin' but."

"They act lak we's the chillren and they's our parents. They ain't nobody's parents. I don't have no intention o' puttin' up with many more weeks o' this and I know the fellers is in agreement."

Roland said, "Don't see how you have any choice. Unless you can swim real well."

"We could take the ship," said Walter.

Roland laughed, curling around to look up at Walter.

"*Take the ship! Take the ship!*" squawked the Ministry of Information.

"Could yew keep that bird quiet?"

"Where would *we* take the ship?" asked Roland, petting the parrot to silence.

"To yer new fewture," said Walter. "We got a worldwide televised audience watchin'. Yew kin have another grab at the glory. Be the Man Who Took the UnderGod from Luther Dorsey."

"His childhood friend," said Roland quietly.

"Zackly."

"I believe that's called mutiny. I don't need any more trouble with the law."

"Kain't commit no mutiny on reality TV. T'ain't real. Any lawyer worth his briefs'd git yew off on it."

"You're serious," said Roland.

"Lak a dog with a bone."

"Why you giving me the handoff? You don't seem to lack for ambition."

"Cause I ain't no natural born leader. These fellers look up to yew."

"Doesn't sound like a good role for me," said Roland, back to lying on his back, eyes closed.

Walter quoted from Homer. "'Shall I live out muh life in uneventful ease? Er die young in battle an' live f'rever on the lips o' poets?' Thass what 'ole Achilles asks hisself and thass a question we all have to answer one time er another. Kain't be avoided."

"I've already answered it," said Roland.

"Life's offerin' a second chance. Yew want to end up like Hector? There's a underdog fer yew. Recall whut happened to him?"

"He died."

"By whut means?"

"At the hand of Achilles."

"Zackly right," said Walter. "An' his body wuz drug round the walls o' the city, his parents lookin' down from the ramparts, sobbin' and renderin' their garments at the awful tragedy of it."

"Zackly," said Roland softly.

Walter said, "I'm gonna offer an observation yew can take note of er not. It ain't much to take a whuppin' an' get drug round the back o' somebody's chariot. It don't make yew any more unusual or poetic than the next feller. I'm lookin' fer a few good men willin' to create their own reality, 'stead of bein' so acceptin' o' this one."

"You're trying to saddle up the wrong horse, Hoss."

Walter said, "Fair enough. But I'll tell yew this, they's plannin' on a mutiny, it's jes a question o' when an' on whose terms an' whut will be the outcome."

"Who's planning a mutiny?"

"Evor Lark. Kain't yew see the star o' this program is big, strong, Luther Dorsey? So the script sez Luther puts down a mutiny. An' Lark recruited me to lead it. Yeah, thass right. Afore we even set sail. He wuz figgerin', quite correckly, I couldn't pull it off. An' Luther'd look like that much more a hero. But they not figgerin' on yew. Yew could take the ship an' the ratin's would bust out an' they'd be writin' 'bout yew in all the magazines at all the supermarkets. Thass a lotta supermarkets. Could git yer own hour-long variety show if yew wanted it. I know I would. I'd like to show off muh dance moves."

Roland said, "Man lives not by fame alone."

"There yew go agin, soundin' all Christ-like. If yew won't do it fer yerself, what about fer the rest of us? That Cape Horn is a tough mother to navigate an' a downright danger to a inexperienced crew. We ain't all gonna make it 'round. We take the ship, we can head fer calmer waters. An' be masterin' our own fate."

"What do you get out of it?" Roland murmured. "Thirty pieces of silver?"

"I don't know whut thass s'posed to mean, but I would urge yew to think on it while yer rollin' around in yer dreamland up here cause things gonna git a whole lot worse afore they gits better. That much I dew know."

* * * * * *

Dinner that evening in the captain's cabin was a cheerful affair; sailors are happier when they're moving forward. After a special dessert of molasses-filled hardtack, the dishes were cleared away. Luther lit a cigar and asked for the report back on the search for evil.

Rob Dawg emptied a duffel bag onto the table: playing cards, cleavage-covered magazines, flasks that once held liquor, a poster displaying the signs of the zodiac and a pair of fuzzy dice that had hung from a carronade.

"Nice haul," said Luther. "You must have learned a lot."

"Mr. Jivens wears a toupee," said Skip.

"And he has false teeth," said Chip.

"And a glass eye," said Skip. "But that could just be for Halloween."

"Jivens," Luther mused. "Whatever happened to him? He was supposed to host the voyage. Haven't seen him in weeks."

"We think he drinks," said Skip.

"He told us absinthe makes the heart grow fonder," said Chip.

Luther said, "Max, see if you can counsel him. What about weapons? Anything?"

Another bag was emptied.

Skip said, "This pair of scissors."

"Careful. Could put somebody's eye out with those."

"A toothbrush with traces of a white, abrasive substance."

Max said, "Too bad we don't have a lab to analyze it."

Chip held up a longish pair of shoe laces. "Strangulation, anyone?"

"Nice job," said Luther. "Is that all?"

Skip said, "Luther sir, before we continue our report, we wanted to be sure you knew the wind has picked up and we're moving forward at a brisk pace—"

"Five, maybe six knots," added Chip.

"How could I not know?" Luther laughed. "It's all from your good work. The Lord is taking action because we've taken action."

Skip said, "You're sure you want to bother with the rest? We know you're busy."

Luther said, "Absolutely. Spill the beans."

Chip stepped forward, chin high, as they'd taught him at the academy. "Sir, we wanted to be fair and above-board in carrying out the assignment. So I searched Skip's room and he searched mine. I found this book underneath Skip's mattress. These passages were underlined and the pages were....pretty well gone over."

He handed a well-thumbed paperback to Luther, who read in haste and then re-read in disbelief.

Luther said, "What the—? A grizzly cub in lace panties and a peek-a-boo nighty? What is this?"

Chip said, "I wasn't exactly sure. I went to Roland, who's seen the seedier side of life. Said he'd come across this sort of thing one summer working in the canneries in Alaska."

"And?"

"It's bear porn."

"Bear porn! Skipper! Why in the blue-eyed world?"

Skip's voice was a whisper. "It seemed weird at first. But I found myself wanting to read it again and again. Now nothing else comes close."

Luther, shocked, dismayed, was also quick to forgive.

"All right son. We each have a soft spot. I myself have been known to linger over the image of a buxom female. Though I manage to stay within my own species. In any case, let's just say we've got a clean slate and move on."

"Thank you, sir," said Skip, shooting a glance at Chip. "Should we continue?"

"Of course."

"It turns out," said Skip, "in Chip's room I found a book taped to the bottom of his writing desk. It also had certain passages highlighted. Have a look for yourself."

Skip handed over the evidence and again Luther's lips moved slowly, uncomprehendingly.

"What? I don't get it!" Luther exclaimed. "Why would someone—? Did you show this to Roland too?"

"We did," said Skip.

"Well?"

"It's deer porn."

"Porn again!?" said Luther. "C'mon! One likes bear porn and one likes deer porn?"

"I got it from a sexaholic I was counseling," said Chip. "She said it would open my eyes. I wish now I could close them again."

"I don't understand," said Luther. "And I'm not sure I want to."

"Deer are so graceful," said Chip.

"But bears have a playful, amorous quality," insisted Skip.

"Guys!" said Luther. "You're supposed to be my knights in shining armor. My warriors in a holy cause. Instead it seems you're obsessed with strange sex. What gives?"

Chip said, "No one feels worse than I do. Permission to fall on my sword?"

"Permission denied," said Luther gruffly. "Chipster, I'll say the same thing to you I said to Skip. You're still my guy. I'm counting on you and so's The Man upstairs."

"I won't let you down again," said Chip.

Luther looked glum.

"So what are you going to tell me about Robbie now? Leopards, lemurs, what?"

"It's nothing like that with Rob," said Skip. "But he does have a matter he'd like to discuss."

"Fine, Rob. What is it?"

"Luther, dawg, sir, I'd rather say it in private. If that's okay."

"Rob, you know Skip, Chip and Max are my inner circle. My most trusted advisers. And you, you're my tiger. If you can say it to me, you can say it to them. Let's have it."

"If that's the way you feel, sir."

"That's the way I feel."

"You know my mamma, she raised me by herself."

"I met her at your graduation. A strong woman."

"She worked two jobs so I could get away from the weezy ho's and dealers settin' up shop. That's behind me now. But I still feel like I gotta represent."

"We're all representing for Jesus," Skip put in.

"Let him talk, Skip," said Chip.

"It's just that Mamma never let me say that word."

"Which word, Rob?" said Luther.

"'Poop'. Whenever we say 'poop deck', we're saying 'poop.'"

Luther squinted, hoping he hadn't understood.

Rob Dawg said, "I just want to keep it real. For her."

Looking like he wanted to shoot himself, Luther said, "Robbie, I appreciate your sensitivity and all but sometimes son, you have to go with the flow. Cover your ears or recite some scripture."

"It is a scatological reference," Max put in. "I don't see why we couldn't say 'aft' or 'stern.' I'll pass the word to the men."

"That would be clutch," said Rob Dawg.

"Done!" said Luther, motioning them into a tight huddle, as in a rugby scrum. Their faces were inches apart.

Luther said, "Look fellas, I'm trying to hold things together down here and I can't afford to sweat the small stuff. Skipper, I'm tasking you to do a better job of sorting things out on your own. Keep these distractions away from me at a time when I'm waging some pretty deep inner battles."

"Got it," said Skip. "Guys, we need to raise our spiritual game to a whole other level."

Rob Dawg vowed, "We need to get right with the Original Gangsta."

"I'm down for that," said Chip fiercely.

"That's it boys," said Luther. "Now give with the love. Hands in. UnderGod on three."

"1-2-3 Un-n-n-n-n-n-derGod!"

Their faith thus renewed, they placed the confiscated tokens of evil back in the bags. As Skip hefted his copy of "Kojo: the Bear Who Played Dress Up", Luther touched his arm.

"Best leave that with me, son," he said.

In front of the assembled crew, the duffel bags filled with evil were tossed over the railing into the ill-rewarded sea. Luther gave a speech pointing out that the wind had turned in their favor within hours of the search for evil. This was no coincidence. The UnderGod had struck a covenant with the Lord in which He would watch over the ship so long as there was strict adherence to His laws.

Roland's tee shirt said "Pump & Dump." Luther looked long and hard, but said nothing.

* * * * * *

Back in the homeland the Voyage of the UnderGod was the center of much controversy. One pundit opined that the UnderGod's crew could well be "making the ultimate campaign contribution—their lives." A nautical historian added, "Proven sailors died rounding Cape Horn in the nineteenth century. And the Cape is even more dangerous now with the severe weather patterns brought on by decades of global warming."

"Don't feel any hotter to me," responded a certain ex-president from his Crawford ranch as his demure wife knitted nearby. "Course I'm always running the AC. But I do think too much is being made about the whys and wherefores of this voyage. The past is behind us. Our boys are on the water and some might not be comin' back. Folks best get behind 'em."

Overseas, opinion was just as divided: *fatwas* were pronounced for and against. Local leaders in drought-stricken east Africa demanded the UnderGod bring them grain. Tiny replicas of the ship appeared in vendors' stalls in Haitian shanty towns, suitable for the pin-sticking of voodoo ritual. The Polish Parliament passed a resolution in support of the Voyage after an almost-identically worded resolution received just two lonely votes at the UN—from the US and Israel.

It took little effort to see the UnderGod as a metaphor for the United States itself, navigating through the treacherous waters of a new millennium. What fate would befall the leader of nations? Could a self-righteous captain, stiff and unyielding, accomplish his mission in the face of a peril perhaps of his own making?

In Brazil a particular fervor arose for the UnderGod as it drew near. In Recife on the continent's easternmost tip, an enormous bonfire was lit in the ship's honor and effigies of witches and goblins thrown onto the flames. At a nearby counter-demonstration, US agricultural protectionism was denounced.

Further south in Bahia, *tribalistas* surged to the shore and waved the ship onward, cheering and dancing at an impromptu outdoor concert which the police could do nothing to stop. And on Copacabana beach in Rio it was pandemonium, the *cariocas* pouring out from the high rise apartments and the wretched *favelas* onto the soft white sand. Bouquets of flowers and personal items of clothing (some quite intimate) were taken to the water's edge and tossed in the surf in hope the tide would drift them out to the celebrated vessel.

On the UnderGod of course, nothing was known of the passions their presence aroused. That first night, gliding past the hump-backed islands dotting the waters of Rio, they could see crowds on the beaches. But it was Rio, they reasoned, so of course there were crowds.

The delay in the doldrums had pushed their arrival back to mid-February, the time of Carnaval. As they weighed anchor the *bom bom bom* of bass drums could be heard, mingled with snatches of riotous song. Contemplating the next day's shore leave, the men realized how badly their personal grooming had deteriorated. They realized they were little better than apelike creatures—hairy, smelly, completely unsuited for a venture into the South American capital of sensuality. They resolved to take corrective action in the morning.

Unable to sleep that night—stimulated by the prospect of Rio—Roland went up on deck to look upon the silhouette of the white-towered city across the broad sweep of the misty bay. He soon found himself in conversation with Braga, who was in a nostalgic mood, reminiscing about this trip to his homeland, which he had not seen in many years.

Braga asked, "Have you ever made love in a hammock?"

"Not yet," said Roland brightly.

"That is how the Rio women make the Portuguese language sound. Their voices have a swaying quality and not far in the background is the act of love. You can listen to them for hours."

Braga placed a hand to his substantial belly and rubbed, as if to conjure up the memories.

"The most beautiful are the mulatos. A mixture of Europeans and native Indians and blacks enslaved from Africa to work the plantations. They have tremendous energy—the whole city does—they call it *movimento*. You see it during Carnaval, which is a frenzy in the best sense of the term. A year of preparation explodes in a single night. The way they dress! I remember a tall, black woman with rounded hips like this, who wore ostrich feathers that tickled my nose as she paraded past in the samba competition. Another had skin I was certain would taste like chocolate, streaks of henna in her hair and a tiny diamond in the curve of a nostril that lent a sparkle to her eyes. For her costume she'd covered her body in lemon-colored spangles. Hundreds. I offered to count them for her."

Braga's lips touched together with delicacy, his eyes expressing at once the pleasure of the memory of desire and the sadness that each day such a memory grew more distant.

"Have you slept with one?" Roland asked.

"I regret to say I have."

"But why regret?"

"I had drunk too much rum and passed out as she was removing my boots and when I woke the next morning she was gone, leaving nothing but that ostrich feather resting on the bed so that its tip still tickled the end of my nose."

In a warm downpour the next morning the men prepared for liberty in earnest, stopping up the scuppers with wet rags, filling the upper decks with stored rainwater. They washed with great cakes of soap, scrubbing each other in boisterous and brotherly affection, telling fantastic stories about Carnaval and what could be done there in a single afternoon, boasting of who would be first to do it. Razors and combs were commandeered. Some fashioned neckties and kerchiefs from spare cloth lying about, as the dandies of old had done.

The rain stopped. They talked in groups, taking in the beauty of the green mountains lining the harbor, asking each moment or so for the time. Ten minutes remained until the first launch was scheduled to leave for shore. Then Max Winter ascended the hatchway in his deliberate, uncertain manner.

"Everyone," he called out in an odd tone that brought quiet at once.

"Disappointing news," he told them. "But I think you'll agree it's for the best in the long run. Luther has cancelled all shore leave. This is Carnaval in Rio and that means too many temptations. We have a lot of spiritual momentum now and we need to keep the Lord on our side. So no leave. That's a final decision. On the bright side, work details will be suspended while we're in harbor so there'll be a little respite for you."

Too stunned to react, the men stared dumbly at their trouser bottoms, the energy they had stored up for Rio leaking out of them in aimless, sideways shuffles. How they had longed to escape the ship's confinement. How they had wanted to feel the earth beneath their feet. To go where they pleased, glance at a tree, linger at a shop window, see a woman, perhaps talk with one, perhaps....

"How about you then? You and Luther? You're going ashore?"

Max said, "Yes. There are meetings with the secular authorities arranged months in advance."

"You go but we don't," came one feeble grumble.

Max said, "You can put that kind of spin on it. But honestly, I was there as Luther agonized over this and he feels awful about it. He had to make a judgment call and he made it and that's—you know, he's the captain. That's his role."

The next few days they took in fresh water and supplies via shuttle runs of the launches, with methodical precautions taken against smuggling. No shore boat could approach without officer-of-the deck approval. Sentries were posted, the most trusted of the crew, standing watch on platforms suspended from the ship's side. Their orders were to fire on any boat persisting in its approach after being hailed. All boarders were frisked at the top of the side ladders, and the UnderGod's officers descended to search each vessel before signaling it be hauled out to the booms for unloading.

The crew resigned itself to seeing Rio only from a distance, and to taste of it only what was brought back in the launches, which is to say the depressingly familiar biscuit flour and salted beef.

A growing minority expressed resentment at being treated like "children." Suspension of the work details was welcome, sure, but how to amuse themselves on board ship? All that remained in the way of historically accurate entertainment were a few checker boards and harmonicas and a box of Bibles and hymnals. So they lounged on deck, gazing with longing at the Rio skyline and the lush greenery, sometimes a lone harmonica letting out a tune tinged with sorrow, sometimes all joining in on a rousing sailing song such as "Gather Round the Turnstile" or "They Done You Wrong, Al Gore."

The last night in harbor, a tossing Roland twisted in his hammock, turning over in his mind how impossible it all was. The *bom bom bom* wafting across the water; he couldn't help thinking of it as an invitation being extended. And by such an alluring host. But to be caught leaving the ship…Roland knew he had pushed Luther as far as he could.

Roland thought of the women as Braga had described them. The mystery of their being, the warm flash of their smiles. He could see them now, a city-full, beckoning, clothed in name only. What was the term Braga had used? *Movimento*.

Roland had sampled much of life but mastered none. He had wandered for too long and he was growing old and he was alone and most likely would stay that way. There was bitterness in him but he had few regrets, and he knew the difference between the two.

He couldn't stand the creaking hammock another second. He went up on deck where the ever-enlarging moon eyed him without remorse. How depressing it all sounded. How lacking in hope. Was there really nothing he loved, as he had said to Luther?

Romantic love was a dimming prospect. Even carnal love came round only rarely now. But there is another love as Melville describes, that radiates from ourselves to the stars, that stirs the orbits of suns we cannot see. The love of everything, of life unadorned. Of this moment, these conical peaks and drooping liana trees and the fantastic pastel-green building on the island in the harbor belonging to the Brazilian Marine Ministry. How not to love all this?

At his age, to be in a position to engage in such an internal debate as he was having, was a marvelous thing. To not have hope in such a situation, Roland decided, was unmanly, lacking in courage.

For who would marvel if he stayed on ship like a mouse in a hole, nibbling at the crumbs of existence? Like a shrub worn down by the adventuresome wind? And if none of us can marvel at any new act of a fellow human being, but only at things already happened, then where was the good in that?

And Roland couldn't radiate any love to the Brazilians unless he was among them. That much was certain.

He waited until the cry for two bells, then a while longer, aiming for the precise moment the sentries' drowsy boredom would be most acute. Poised at a porthole, he eased into the water with pointed toes and upraised arms. The barest ripple. He swam beneath the surface. Coming up, he faced away from the UnderGod so his breathing would not be heard. He could have been a buoy or a coconut shell drifting in the calm, warm harbor.

He made for the bright lights of Copacabana and rode the surf to shore, presenting a startling sight to the exhausted lovers embracing on the illustrious sand. Lacking a single *cruzeiro*, possessed of only a smattering of Portuguese, he was nevertheless at liberty.

Dodging desultory traffic, he crossed the wide Avenida Atlantica, lined with palms and covered in its slithering, patterned mosaic. He flirted with the idea of not returning to the ship. But his passport was onboard. Could he claim political asylum from a TV show? Doubtful.

He noticed first the wailing of sirens coming close and going away and the controlled panic of the car alarms, as in any megalopolis when night is gone and morning not yet arrived. Shops and windows were brightly lit, since the dark could not be trusted. In the restaurants and sidewalk cafes facing the ocean the scattered patrons were tanned, elegant, sipping coffee, dipping strips of steak in pepper sauce and making weary, chewing motions.

Roland's fate was to have chosen the morning of Ash Wednesday for his lone visit to Rio. The debaucheries of Carnaval were over; now was the beginning of Lent and repentance. Everywhere in the streets and at the bases of the towering buildings was debris: trampled streamers, samba song sheets soaked in beer. A powdered wig. A spaceman's ray gun.

He surged ahead, hoping to make something happen; but the best he could do was a stop at a newspaper kiosk, and then in a hotel lobby for a halting conversation with three look-alike security guards in uniforms with faux gold trim.

He stood before a tapestry hung in a department store window, a scene from the colonial past in which a beggar sought alms while supported on a stretcher by a quartet of slaves. In the next window he saw a swan with curving neck sculpted in marble, and in the next an aquarium with brightly colored fish, some darting, some still.

Women's voices came from behind him. There were two. One seemed drunk, the other not so much. The taller, not-so drunk one gave the other a bump in Roland's direction with her not inconsiderable hips and then pretended someone up ahead was calling her and hurried off.

The girl remaining with Roland seemed very happy to see him and stood close, touching and giving little squeezes to his shoulders and grabbing onto his arms and making little beckoning movements and her scent was unforgettable, a mixture of youth and perfume and at least one person's desire and Roland thought for a moment he must have met her before until he realized the over-friendliness meant they were probably on camera and that the girl was working from a script in which it was written she would seduce Roland Orr.

Of course. An Opticon camera must have spotted him. The cameras were everywhere. A runaway crew member in Rio would be a big episode in the Voyage of the UnderGod. Well-advertised.

Not that that was necessarily a deal-breaker. The world's a stage in which we all play our parts, from whatever motives we can muster. No one believed that more than Roland. The whole thing might have gone off fine except when she thought he wasn't looking, Roland's glance caught a flicker on the girl's face of utter disinterest, and it was then Roland allowed himself to see her unformed youth, and the vast distance separating them, and how truly commercial was the transaction they were about to consummate.

And Roland surprised himself when he said to her, "no thanks" and shook his head in refusal and headed back for the beach over her howls of disappointment, which were real but not in the way they pretended to be.

As he walked Roland tried to make sense of this sudden reversal in his thinking. He might have gone through with it if he hadn't thought someone was watching. He wasn't sure who that someone was, and why it mattered, and whether the watcher was inside him or outside him. A disembodied voice perhaps. He wanted to think more but time was running out and his thinking got all tangled up in the concepts of God and conscience and camera and then he passed by a department store, its display window stacked with televisions, each broadcasting an image of Roland in front of that same department store looking at those same televisions. He'd guessed right about the camera. He stood for an indulgent moment, watching himself being watched. All the little Rolands lined up in a row.

The sky was beginning to lighten. He had a look around for who could be filming. That man smoking across the street—judging by the angle, it had to be him.

Taking off at a trot he showed the man his middle finger, and Roland pictured in his mind the display window behind him full of middle fingers lined up in a row, and he gave a grateful smile as he ran down the beach into the Rio dawn spreading before him like a banquet he couldn't stay to enjoy. Plunging into the surf, he made for the UnderGod anchored at the mouth of the bay, bare spars standing out amid the rusting old tankers and massive cargo ships. Getting close, he swam underwater, but when he rose for air he was just short of a hanging platform, looking directly up into a sentry's eyes.

The alarm was sounded and Roland powered for the nearest porthole as a bullet splished in the water nearby. He hoisted himself through and scrambled up a ladder to the forecastle, and grabbed whatever material was available to dry his hair and then put on a dry shirt and climbed carefully into his hammock so it wouldn't rock too much. He closed his eyes and pretended to sleep but that parrot—that infernal green bird he'd named the Ministry of Information—couldn't stop squawking and fluttering, stimulated by his master's sudden return.

They came in seconds later. There were scores of hammocks to search but they had only to follow the sound of the bird and Roland felt a hand on his still-wet clothing and heard Rob Dawg's voice say, "What up, my nizzle? Early morning swim?" Roland pretended to be waking, but there was no hiding it, and they laughed and said, "Polly want a cracker?" and laughed some more. Roland was caught in the act; it was the same old story.

They brought him to Luther's cabin; Luther wasn't happy being woken so early. He sat on the edge of the bed in a striped robe, ruffling his disheveled hair. Rob Dawg had Roland by the arm.

Luther said, "You can let him go."

"Thanks Chief," said Roland.

"Skip it. You know, you've pulled one too many of these stunts. I'm going to have to come down on you, or they'll all start doing what they please. Why can't you follow the rules?"

Roland said, "It's not the end of the world."

Luther said, "Don't joke about the end of the world. It'll happen sooner than you think." Luther ruffled his hair again. "Did you think about what would happen if you got caught?"

"As a matter of fact, I did."

"It doesn't seem like it. Unless you're trying to be a martyr. That's what I think, sometimes. That you're not what you seem to be at all."

"What is it I seem to be?"

"Happy-go-lucky Roland. Laughable Roland, affable Roland. But you're really a manipulator. You're forcing me to make you a martyr."

"How can I force you to do something?"

"I don't know," said Luther, his head buried in his hands. "It's like I'm being dragged along against my will and you, you're part of it. Don't look so smug. Max, I need some Maalox. My stomach is killing me. Take him out of here.

"And I hope we'll be able to find him when we need him," Luther added, shooting a sharp look at the grinning Rob Dawg.

"He won't leave my sight," said Rob Dawg, pleased with his assignment.

Roland said, "Does this gorilla have to follow me around?"

Rob Dawg flashed his gold-toothed smile.

"You're the gorilla," he said to Roland. "You believe in evolution."

V

THEY SAILED SOUTH FROM RIO and the officers noted an increase in suspicious conversations and sluggishness in carrying out orders. The word 'mutiny' was carefully avoided but Luther directed that officers carry loaded pistols and enforce discipline with the 'colt': a short, knotted piece of rope that could be used like a blackjack.

Roland's sentence was a week of confinement, on bread and water rations. Luther forbade communication between Roland and the rest of the crew. He was placed in irons behind a gun-carriage on the main deck port side, where he could be looked after by the officer-in-charge.

The weather still warm, Roland slept intermittently through the first night, eyeing the star-drenched sky that served as a backdrop to the great sheets of canvas that were the UnderGod's glory. Bread and water wasn't too inspiring but he could take it for a week. And he received the occasional encouraging word when the officer-in-charge was otherwise occupied.

But the second day the craving came over him. He had no access to his opium. By day three his eyes teared up and he was sweating, racked with chills, nauseous. The weather turned cooler and he asked for an extra blanket. It grew cooler still as they approached what Braga told them was the coast of Uruguay.

Luther, informed of Roland's apparent sickness, said it was a ploy to get his punishment reduced. When it persisted, Luther went up to see for himself. Roland, chained, sat hunched with arms around his knees, quietly shaking.

"What are you, cold?" said Luther.

"Not exactly."

"You don't look good. I'll have them bring another blanket."

"You're a prince."

Luther stood over him. "And you're a real dead-ender. Some day you'll stop playing the joker and face up to what life really is."

"What is it, really?"

"A chance to serve. You know, Dorsey Ministries provided more than a million meals to African children last year."

Roland said, "I've got no quarrel with that."

"Then what is it you're quarrelling with?"

"Invisible gods."

"God's presence would blind you if you'd permit yourself to see Him. What's keeping you from seeing Him?"

"I suspect it's His non-existence."

"Really? How did we get here, then? Out of all the worlds in the universe, is it a coincidence we're on this one?"

"I don't know."

"That's not much of an answer."

"Not all questions have answers."

Luther laughed at Roland's absurd reply. "I can't very well stand before my congregation saying, 'I don't know'. You're so wrapped up in yourself, you've lost sight of the bigger picture." Luther turned to go. No arguing with a stubborn, withdrawn little soul. Pity made him turn back again.

"Pray with me," he said on an impulse, at once pleading and commanding.

Roland shook his head.

"Scripture tells us when the Devil has his claws in a man, he's incapable of prayer," said Luther.

"Scripture's right about that one," said Roland with a shiver.

Walter was mopping the deck one morning around the still-shaking Roland.

"I see yer in the grasp o' yer fiendish drug addiction."

"I'm quitting for good. I'll never go through this again."

"Uh-huh. That tune's familiar enuff I could tap muh feet to it. Have yew given any thought to muh proposition, now that yew've bin chained like a animal to a post?"

"It's not so bad being chained to a post. In some ways it's a more straightforward way to be."

"Suitcherself. It's startin' to get downright chilly at night. Judgin' from the purple in yer lips, I'd say yew'd want to git out o' this situation pronto, one way or t'other."

"Tonight's my last night. Then I'm a free man."

"Free to stay on board an' follow ever order they dole out to yew."

"I guess freedom isn't free. Isn't that what they're always saying?"

"Yep. I hear it oftener an' oftener."

They passed the wide expanse where the Rio de la Plata empties into the sea in a milky-white swirl. At Braga's request they fired off the long guns in honor of Buenos Aires, where he said he'd once danced a tango with the only woman in a bar full of men with daggers.

They made their final preparations for the squally Cape that awaited. Light sails replaced with a more durable canvas. The yards set well and taut, the backstays fitted, the fore and main braces rove anew so they might have time to stretch and become limber before the coldest weather made such adjustments impossible.

They beat down the coast of Argentina. Cold ocean currents pushed up at them now in earnest, and the jungle landscape along the seldom-glimpsed shoreline was gone, replaced by low, windswept scrub. At night the nebulae known as the Magellan Clouds dusted the horizon of the southern sky. Braga pointed out four sharp points of light that formed an elongated, tilted diamond shape: the Southern Cross.

One afternoon found Luther with looking glass in hand, observing the action up close as Chip Ribbons directed a gunnery drill. There being no targets in the surrounding sweep of ocean, evaluation could be made only in terms of the frequency with which the guns were made to shoot.

Luther spotted a distant grouping of rocks on which a covey of gulls was perched, and several black seals sunned themselves rather inelegant-ly. Pointing, he handed his glass to Chip Ribbons and said, "How's that for a bull's-eye?"

Chip said, "Aye-aye, sir," and gave crisp instruction to the gunnery crew. In seconds iron balls were sent hissing across the sea.

Max Winter appeared at Luther's side.

"Too long," said Luther. "They didn't budge."

"Luther," said Max. "We need to talk. Right away."

"In a minute," said Luther.

Chip ordered an adjustment. There ensued another round of loading and ramming, striking of the match and covering of the ears.

"Closer," said Luther, peering. "The gulls have fled but the seals are unmoved. They seem to sense no danger."

"Luther, it's important," said Max.

"Here's one for you, Satan," Chip muttered, after another adjustment had been communicated to the hard-laboring gunners.

Another bone-shaking explosion.

"Ha!" Luther cried. "Blood and blubber! Blood and blubber! Nice shooting, men."

"We've got the devil on the run now," said Chip, allowing himself a grin.

"What is it Max?" said the still-pleased Luther after the two had ascended a series of companion ladders to the quarter deck.

"I've just spoken with Walter Pickett. He told me there's a mole on board ship, planted here by Evor Lark to try to lead a mutiny against you."

Luther stopped. "Why would Evor Lark do such a thing?"

"For the ratings, Pickett says. Lark's always stressing the importance of dramatic conflict, isn't he?"

"Yes. Yes he is. This is a serious charge Pickett is making."

Max said, "I can't imagine him deceiving us. He seems so authentic."

"But why would Lark have told Pickett? If it's intended to be a secret?"

"He said Lark had let it slip during a phone call as they made last minute arrangements about his participation. Walter hates being a snitch. But he felt he couldn't go any longer without telling us."

"And who is this mole supposed to be?" Luther asked, steadying himself for the blow.

Max said, "He doesn't know. Only that there's a mole."

Luther said, "I don't consider Pickett's accusation definitive proof. But a pattern starts to emerge. Perhaps I don't want to believe a certain person to be capable of certain things. We'll keep an ear to the ground on this one. I wish I could get through to Saul."

At the weekly review Luther went from sailor to sailor, critiquing their attire in detail, noting infractions as Skip Robbins made notes. They'd been standing on point nearly an hour as a cold wind played against their faces and the choppy seas covered them with spray sweeping over the sides.

In the last row was Roland, his tee shirt reading 'Small is Beautiful'.

Arriving before him, Luther's eyes flashed fire. He shouted, "No!" as if a private dialogue had been interrupted. "I disagree!"

Luther strode to the front of the formation in an arm-swinging gait like an angry bear awoken from slumber, like an offensive line coach gone amok. He blew a whistle he had taken to hanging from his neck.

His voice magnified by a speaking trumpet, Luther said, "Let me point out to you something that should already be apparent. This isn't the Voyage of the Tiny, Harmless Ship. Feel this deck. Touch these masts. They're not made from recycled materials. This is the UnderGod. The real deal. Small is beautiful? Try shock and awe, baby. That's how the west was won. Think big and you act big.

"Some people don't study history. They don't seem to notice God placed the United States at the top of the food chain. It's not a coincidence and it's not a bad place to be either. So the message is this: get on board or get out of the way.

"Roland Orr. Because of your continued insubordination in the form of meaningless slogans and cute remarks you go out of your way to display on your clothing, I sentence you to flogging." He paused, red-faced, wondering at their quiet attention, growing suspicious of it.

"A single lash," he said. "Not with a whip, just the....punishment this afternoon! Maybe that will get your attention. Maybe that will get everyone's attention. I hope there are no questions. Good. You're dismissed."

In the afternoon those not on watch went below for a sleep, but the main hatchway flew open in a trice and a summons rang through the forecastle: "All hands witness punishment ahoy!" They filed back up on deck, curiosity mixing with unease.

There Luther waited. He called out, "Bring up the prisoner." A delay, then a path cleared and they led Roland to the center of the solemn gathering. He was wearing a long-sleeved, checked shirt unmarred by ironic messaging.

Luther read from notes in a business-like tone, as if conducting a foreclosure auction. "Roland Orr. Under the powers vested in me by the Precepts Corporation and in performance of my duties as captain of the UnderGod and in recognition of your continual, habitual insubordination, the details of which have been placed in the captain's log and made a part of the official history of this voyage, I hereby command your punishment to begin. A single lash from the whip. Remove the prisoner's upper garments."

Roland's checked shirt was taken off, revealing a tee shirt he wore underneath that read 'God is Watching.'

A standoff ensued then between the two old playmates: Roland, hands tied, poker-faced, tranquil even, giving nothing away. Luther in flushing face, his mind working furiously, anger vying with a voice in his head warning him not to fall into whatever trap Roland was setting.

"Sentence is amended," Luther said finally with a little toss of his head. "Make it half a dozen."

Skip Robbins and Chip Ribbons then bound Roland's feet to the crossbars and raised his arms to tie his hands to the netting above and now he hung from the netting and at a grim nod from Luther, Rob Dawg advanced, using the fingers of his left hand to comb out the nine tails of his cat-whip, sweeping the cat up around his neck and bringing it down onto Roland's back six times in succession. The prisoner took punishment in silence, mostly, emitting a kind of whispered response to the final two blows and hanging his head at the last. He was sent below to have the wounds looked after.

This was a change in tone. Instead of resuming their duties, the men milled about. The officers went among them, alternately cajoling and scolding, resorting finally to questioning. Why did those on watch not take up the assigned tasks? Why did others engage in the wasting of leisure time? Other punishments awaited other insubordinations, make no mistake about it, they said with as much foreboding as they could muster.

Still the men remained in place, delaying the return to normalcy which would have implied nothing had happened. When an officer approached they turned away or lowered their eyes and didn't seem to hear. Each command required repetition or else the men didn't seem to understand what was wanted.

Walter Pickett went from group to group talking earnestly, paying most attention to the gunnery crew.

Only with great difficulty did the officers eventually succeed in bringing about the resumption of routine vital to a ship at sea.

They continued south under scowling skies, seas rolling high with white-topped swells. One bleak and awful morning the lookout raised a cry of "Land ho!" and pointed to the larboard quarter, where they saw in the distance two mountainous islands. These were the Falklands. And somehow, as if in possession of a secret periscope a ghostly figure appeared on deck at that very moment, barefoot, in belt-less pants and a wispy cotton gown covered in stains of unknown provenance. It was Stanley Jivens, pasty, emaciated, reeking of strong-smelling hair oil. He lurched to the railing and gazed out at the barren humps of land.

"There's the glory," he said to no one in particular through the soon-uncontrollable chatter of his false teeth. Pointing, he saluted. As if there were a flag.

"Not on Margaret Thatcher's watch," he muttered in dogged affirmation, overwhelmed now by the frigid air, turning to go back down below but as he did so tripping on his trouser pants, which had slid to his ankles. He pitched forward, opening a cut to his chin where it struck the ship's deck. He sat up slowly, dazed. There was something horrible about him. No one went to help.

"Basra too," Jivens concluded, still in a mutter. "Tony was right. God will judge. He will decide."

Then he vanished down below.

The islands sank away to the northeast as the UnderGod entered the waters of Tierra del Fuego—Land of Fire—given its name by Magellan, historians say, when he mistook lightning striking the empty, windswept land for human-made fire. Some historians have no sense of irony.

Fogs and vapors drew close round the pitching ship. The seas became oily smooth, a low swell rolling under the surface, lifting and lowering the UnderGod in a rhythm of deep respiration. Roland, with bandaged back, took his turn on the midnight watch, seeking in vain for a star's comforting light, seeing only blackness, feeling the chill air and the ship's not-so-gentle rocking.

He began to doze despite an uneasy feeling that should have kept him awake. There was increasing cold. Roland felt he must be dreaming because it seemed the sea was now coming alive, that he could sense its breathing in drawn-out sighs. He felt surrounded—and he knew that feeling well.

He started at a shrill scream. Animal or human? From outside the ship? Yet what cruel murder could take place in such desolation? More noises followed, strange, unfathomable—to which he tried to assign a meaning, as any human would. A vague cacophony he heard as the jumble and clatter of children's voices shouted from a playground somewhere in the distance. A creaking groan he turned into an old song. And that bellowing—as if an army of mad cattle were adrift in these unattainable seas.

Hours later, with the surrounding fog suffused in the light of a dull dawn he made out dark forms floating in the water and soon saw the truth of the situation: the UnderGod was in the midst of a pod of bowhead whales. It was their breathing he had heard during the night, and the blowing of their spray. Bowhead whales are known to make a variety of sounds, for reasons humans do not understand.

The men took their breakfast below deck, where it was warmer. They came up and talked quietly in the presence of the whales, who seemed to be staying close to the ship. A restlessness on board was growing, a nervousness as in athletes before a competition, or defendants awaiting a pitiless judgment.

Max Winter watched with unease as Braga manned the stern and tacked ship into the wind and steered clear of the occasional ice chunk appearing in their path. They were still among the bowheads, which seemed to have taken an interest in the ship and its occupants.

Max said, "Some of them seem to be paired up."

Braga flashed his big grin, all gums and teeth.

"It takes two to tango," Braga said. "The bulls are always in the mood for love."

Max said, "Goodness. I suppose in a way this is their bedroom, isn't it?"

Braga said, "And we're peeking through the window."

"That's a funny way of putting it."

Braga said, "All men who love life are voyeurs."

Max peered through a glass. "They're enormous creatures."

"Whales have great fortitude," Braga agreed, eyeing the waters ahead. "In fact they can sink a ship. One of your whaling vessels in the nineteenth century sailed from Nantucket. There's an exciting book about it. It was rammed by a bull sperm whale in the Pacific and sank.

The survivors floated in the ship's boats to the coast of Chile more than four thousand miles away. They had to resort to cannibalism to survive."

"How awful."

"And then there's Moby Dick. That white whale destroyed a ship and a man's soul as well."

The wind, picking up, slapped at their faces.

Max said, "Yes, but Moby Dick isn't true. It's fiction."

"Many parts were true," said Braga. "Melville had sailed on a whaling vessel. He knew a great many things about the sea."

"But the part about the white whale," Max persisted. "That was invented."

"There are white whales," replied Braga. "We may see some yet. They're called belugas and they swim with their babies on their backs. I've sometimes heard them make strange sounds, like birds chirping. In fact I heard some last night."

"But the white whale called Moby Dick," Max said doggedly. "He didn't really exist."

"Keep your voice down," said Braga. "They can hear you."

Luther, who'd quietly joined them, said, "It seems our captain is having his fun with you Max. He wants us to believe whales possess greater powers than in fact they do."

"I think that is right," said Braga. "That is what I want you to believe. Because you do not give Nature its proper respect."

Luther said, "God has given Nature to us. He has not given us to Nature."

Braga said, "When we round the Cape, there will be no question of who is being given to whom."

Braga called up to the lookout for a report on an object ahead. Only more ice. Max went forward to reprimand an idle sailor.

Braga said, "Luther, you've taken us to the ends of the earth. If we go any further to the south, we will have to use dogs to move forward instead of sails. To accomplish our mission."

Braga chuckled. He was invigorated by the foul weather and the adventure of their situation. Luther was drawn and sober, acutely aware of the burdens of leadership.

The lookout cried out for land off the starboard bow. Another bare and broken island—jagged rock and ice coated in a stubborn, stunted vegetation. This was Staten Land.

An escalating wind snapped the sails above them; the skies grew dimmer still.

"The ends of the earth," said Braga as if calling out the stops on a tour bus. "Tell me Luther, how it all will end? Fire or water? Looks like it could be ice. What does the good book say?"

"In ways not unlike those we are now experiencing," Luther replied. "Wars and rumors of wars. The sun will veil itself and the moon will darken. The angels will gather the Elect from the four winds. The graves will open and the saints will tread upon the stars. This earth will pass away."

"Spoken like a true madman," said Braga. "I knew we could find some common ground."

"The difference between us Braga is I believe in the truth of what I just described because it is in the Bible. Whereas you I suppose took my words as metaphor only."

"True enough," said Braga. "Too bad. We were getting along so well. Then tell me this, is it possible to use your videophone or whatever name you have for it. You see, it's my mother. She lives in New York and I want to inquire about her health."

"Only I am permitted communication with the homeland," said Luther, clasping his hands firmly behind him and swaying front to back on his heels.

"But for the sake of an old woman who may be dying," said Braga. "Won't you let her speak to her son?"

"I'll place her foremost among my prayers," said Luther, hoping to make Braga understand. "Every man wants one kind of exception or another. I have to enforce the laws of this voyage without playing favorites."

Their eyes met.

"Just do your job, Braga. Leave the rest to the Lord. And to me."

Braga said, "It will take all of us doing our job. We cannot be divided against ourselves. Or the Cape will destroy us."

They sailed the rest of the day in icy blue enchantment, well to the south of Staten Land. At night came racing clouds and behind them glimpses of a pale, forsaken moon.

VI

BY MORNING THE WIND blew not from the south but the west, and with a heightened bitterness. They were at the Cape at last. Braga ordered loose items on the upper decks lashed securely and the main deck guns run in and housed. Portholes were closed off, yards hauled in, the booms made fast. They inched forward, the mainsail and main topgallant the only sail they carried.

The lookout cried for a ship and they stole glances at it, even as they shunned it. An enormous cargo vessel bearing close upon them from the west, under an unidentifiable flag, carrying containers the size of city buildings. Filled with automobiles perhaps, or refrigerators stacked like matchsticks. This ship, they knew, had engine rooms, dining rooms. Break rooms with sofas and satellite TV. And a steel hull. It dwarfed them in passing and disappeared to the east, leaving them to their frailties and their doubts.

At the mid-day meal Luther appeared on deck, his mood altered from the day before. Now he paced like a lion, encouraging the men to their duties, trying to rouse them from their fearful languor, shaking a man or his mate or the both of them by the collar to emphasize a particular command.

Failing to effect a change in morale, he ordered Rob Dawg to fire off two of the long guns in a gesture of defiance, a way of bringing heat and noise into play. The exertion of human will against forces beyond its control.

Hands on hips, Luther stood like an oriental satrap waiting to see and hear the carrying out of his command. But no sound came from the gun deck below. Rob Dawg reported back on the trot that the long guns had been sabotaged: the breechings had been cut. By whom the gunnery crew could not say, but Luther felt no need for their expertise.

He had his own opinion.

Down the main hatchway he tumbled in a rage, entering with a burst into the forecastle where those not on watch were occupied in one or another meager form of entertainment. Skip, Chip and Rob followed on his heels.

"Where's Roland Orr? Which is Roland Orr's?"

Startled to alertness, the men pointed to the far corner where Roland slept, the Ministry of Information nearby in his cage, cherry head bobbing in excitement at the sudden commotion.

"*Br-a-a-a-a-ck. Br-a-a-a-a-ck. Pieces of eight. Pieces of eight,*" said the parrot.

Roland sat up, heels of his hand rubbing at his face.

Luther's anger was building. "What do you know about the guns? The truth."

Roland gave a sleepy mumble.

"The guns," Luther repeated.

"Don't know what you want from me," Roland repeated.

"*Where's the treasure? Where's the treasure?*" squawked the parrot, practically in Luther's ear.

"I'm asking again. There's been deliberate sabotage. I think you were involved."

Roland shook his head, arms resting on thighs, wrists dangling between his legs. "Don't know bout no sab-o-taj-ee," he said.

Suddenly Rob Dawg made a grab for Roland's kit bag.

"Hey!" said Roland, wrestling for possession of the bag. Some of its contents spilled out: a comb, a hand mirror, a rubber. And a half-empty plastic packet holding a white powder.

"I ain't Miss Cleo," said Rob Dawg, opening the packet. "But I know this ain't sugar." He dipped his finger in and tasted.

"It's for pain," said Roland as the Ministry of Information made hopeless hops along his thin stick of a perch.

Luther said, "There'll be no problem as long as you can show us a doctor's prescription."

"It's self-medication," said Roland.

"*Chick*enhawk! *Chick*enhawk!" screeched the parrot.

Luther turned to Rob. "How did he get this through the drug screening?"

Rob Dawg said, "Roland didn't go through no drug screen. Dude from Opticon said he didn't have to."

"*Chick*enhawk! *Chick*enhawk! *Chick*enhawk! *Chick*enhawk!"

When the Ministry of Information became excited, he tended to repeat himself. Luther took sudden note of his avian accuser and banged the bird's cage in anger. The bird went silent as the cage remained swinging from the force of Luther's blow.

"You taught him that!" Luther said, pointing to Roland.

"Take it easy Luther, he's only a parrot," said Roland in an annoyed tone as he tried to soothe the shaken bird.

"About me. Your friend. Your supposed friend. You taught him…that."

Luther could feel their stares, feel how the focus had shifted. He knew dimly that somewhere a camera was rolling. He spoke in defensive tones, as if to a larger, unseen audience.

"It isn't as simple as a mocking little phrase makes it seem. I wanted to serve. There were other priorities. I had more options than most. Am I to be blamed for that? For someone of my patriotic temperament, it's especially tragic, this situation. But I've never made an issue of it. Never paraded my pain for public consumption. Now to be confronted with this…the politics of personal destruction. It's too much. Too much."

"*Chick*enhawk! *Chick*enhawk!" screamed the Ministry of Information in defiance.

"Take them both!" Luther demanded. Rob Dawg snatched the bird while Skip and Chip bundled Roland into his pea coat and hustled him up onto the main deck.

There they were greeted with a scene of surpassing strangeness. Directly overhead a hole had opened among the gathering clouds. The slate-grey sky that had weighed upon them now held in its middle a delicate patch of blue sparkling above. An unexpected blue, like the color of Christ's eyes when first you gaze upon them.

The sun, lately but a pale copper presence, vague and uncaring, shone unobstructed through this wondrous gap, its rays a kiss on their upturned faces. The wind, which had stung like scorn, had died away. Utterly becalmed, they could only watch as their breath emerged into the sharp cold air and disappeared. How close the angels felt. How kind their smiles.

For this brief moment there was this brief hope: that all the talk in the books of nautical history was exaggeration. Perhaps too the severe weather patterns scientists were always going on about were a hoax. Or it could be that the nasty weather had been drawn away to another part of the earth so that the previously ruinous Cape Horn would greet them now with flowers and sweets.

And topple before them in surrender.

Such hope is delicate, like bubbles on the surface of prematurely poured champagne. As it turned out the patch of blue would vanish as quickly as it appeared. It was a freak of sorts. To realize this they had only to look ahead at the dark doom bearing down upon them in the form of thickening black clouds to the west heaped atop one another, extending downward to merge with the roiling seas, blotting out the horizon. Eager to accomplish their mission, these clouds, desirous of expressing their severity.

The air began to stir. Then the laughing wind resumed.

The skies darkened; seabirds fled inland with shrill cries. The seas rose around the ship in gawky swells. The men of the UnderGod remained rooted in place, in their weather-ready jackets and woolen caps and pathetic, historically accurate mittens.

The storm hit them where they stood.

The first gusts snapped the mainsail back against the center mast with a sound like a rifle shot. Braga shouted commands. The swells grew to green walls of water and came crashing down, seemingly at a time of their choosing. The seas burst in through the hawse-holes and over the knight-heads and the rolling of the decks caused the bows to dip below the water in a way that was terrifying.

The covering of the main hatch was pried open, letting in the noisy tumult. The call of "All hands on deck!" was sent down. But the ship's lean was so severe the ladders could only be ascended with difficulty. Arriving on deck it wasn't clear to the men what purpose was served by their presence: with the seas washing over the sides and sometimes down from above, it was all they could do to find a rope or rail to grasp onto, so as not to be swept into the watery void.

"Topmen! Aloft! Haul up the mainsail!"

Thus did Braga cry out; for the wide mainsail was catching the full force of the furious wind and flattening down against the mainmast in spasms, thereby intensifying the terrible strain. They could hear the mainmast's groaning as it fought to maintain its rightful position as the centerpiece of the ship.

"Topmen! Aloft! Haul up the mainsail! Or it will be the end of us all!"

Thus did Braga call into the howling wind. Skip Robbins had to push them by the backside up the rigging, castigating as cowards those refusing to carry out the command. The bravest among them managed to make the ascent and, forming human chains, they laid out along the mainsail yard to haul in the massive, rain-soaked canvas, keeping in touch all the while, via an arm or hooked ankle to the man next to them.

Hastily gathering the sail into folds, they secured it to the stays and lashed it as best they could, inching meekly back in, trembling from fear and cold, making grateful descent to the deck below.

Without delay a new danger presented itself: the main topgallant had worked loose and was being blown to leeward in a crazy flapping rhythm. The main mast was still in danger. The topgallant had to be taken in or cut away.

Hailstones mixed now with the rain. The gusts picked up intensity. Those few who dared venture above the sheltering bulwarks felt immediately the full force of the blasting wind. Each who attempted to ascend the rigging—now coated with newly-forming ice—was driven off in defeat.

Roland and Luther huddled round the capstan as Braga came over, slipping and crawling and shouting to Luther, "Someone must go up! Order them! They must obey you!"

Luther eyed the ropes. He had seen them all try and fail: Skip and Chip, Rob Dawg. His stalwarts.

Observing his friend's dilemma with keen interest was the still-bandaged Roland, the consummate anti-hero who, like most of his kind, had a soft spot for the lone act of heroism.

Roland could feel their eyes on him, expectant, admiring, hoping he would…but no that wasn't right. No one's eyes were on him. It was all they could do to keep from being swept into the drowning sea. Only Luther was looking at him, a look with several different kinds of recognition and fear.

Up on his feet, Roland shouted into the storm as if playing a part in a movie that would turn into a cult classic one day: "Captain! Valiant captain! I'll save the ship!" Then he was off, as Luther called after him, arms flailing like a marionette, "No! You're a prisoner! I forbid you!"

Crawling the short distance to the foot of the mainmast, Roland inched upward, absorbing the blow whenever a risen wave met the lean of the ship, trying always to keep his back to the shifting wind so its force would blow him back into the rigging, to which he clung like a new-born and whose swaying grew more schizoid the higher he went.

Little to note about the ascent other than a reckless moment as he tore a hand loose to find his knife and slash the topgallant free. Then the treacherous descent, which any mountaineer knows is always the more difficult and dangerous. Exhausted at the end, numbed fingers gave way and Roland dropped the final feet, trusting in those who waited to catch him.

They had crowded round to be there, touch him in gratitude. They held Roland with care, his eyes were closed, his limp body draped among them serpentine, completely at rest. They rushed him below for warm blankets and hot tea.

Some remained on deck, attempting whatever scant adjustments could be made to thwart the will of the storm. And so the UnderGod alternated between riding atop the highest waves and wallowing in their trough. And thus ill-treated did it go plunging through the heaving seas of Cape Horn.

* * * * * *

In his cabin under a dim swinging lamp, in the prolonged act of switching from wet clothes to dry, Luther sat in long johns, massaging the toes of one foot over and over again and again, pondering.

Oh there was undermining under way. No doubt of that now. It was a power play, wasn't it? To rally the men to a mutinous cause.

Not what he appeared to be at all, his Roland, this Roland, dashing, so daring, full of bravery and charisma in the service of what end? He, Luther, more of a plodder, a man of the people. The common touch. That's all he had. The only gift he'd been given.

It did no good to sit brooding like this. He thought of going wandering among the ship's mysterious lower regions.

He would go! On a sort of fact-finding tour, poking his head in the sail rooms as they did their mending, having a look round the sick bay, lingering over Roland's bunk to express his concern. Maybe a lighthearted trip through the galley, tasting the soup, yuk! What's in there? Old shoes? Ha ha. Then to the shot room where iron balls were piled in pyramids.

Perhaps a word to the stout lad cleaning the cables: How is it today with you, Sailor? Going to be rough going the next few weeks. Be sure to say your prayers. What's that? Of course I remember the song. The tinkling tune the ice cream truck played long ago those long summer evenings rolling through the neighborhood sending us running to mom and dad to ask for a quarter. Popsicle, please. Popsicles for everyone!

Then somehow Max was there, good old Maxie, taking him by the arm, leading him back to his cabin, telling him to rest, that it did no good to wander the ship in such a state, as if he needed to have that explained to him. Who did they think he was?

Luther Dorsey, that's who: a leader, a shepherd keeping faith with his flock, a shining light in shiny long johns. They get that way after they've been worn a bit. Everybody knows that.

Sleeping until noon, Luther woke refreshed, determined on a course of action. After a brief conference with Max and Rob Dawg, Roland was again brought up on deck. The storm had abated, though the weather remained foul.

Rob Dawg carried a piece of heavy canvas about four feet long and wide enough to go around a man's body. It had long pockets sewn in it and in these they placed Roland's arms as he was made to lie face down on the deck. Rob laced the canvas up in the back, giving a few extra tugs to make it nice and snug. Then they rolled the gasping Roland over and covered him with blankets and a rain slicker.

"You won't be able to go on your drug trips now," said Luther.

"Can't breathe," said Roland, struggling to speak.

"Perhaps now you'll tell us about those guns."

Roland said they were crazy, at which they laughed.

Max said, "The strait jacket is the most effective command and control technology ever invented. Nothing electronically-based approaches it. And it's very affordable."

"Doesn't sound crazy to me," said Luther. A round-the-clock guard was posted, to prohibit all contact between Roland and the rest of the crew.

Questioned by the men about Roland's punishment, the officers replied there were things that couldn't be told, that Roland needed to be observed at all times. For his own good and that of the ship. Braga was outraged but had his hands full navigating among the potentially fatal ice islands now dotting the sea around them.

"Point out to them that he's just lying there," said Luther, reclining in his cabin, when apprised of the crew's concerns. "It's a lot like I'm doing now. What's so torturous about this?"

The Cape's fierce weather curtailed the crew's normal activities. Accustomed to promenading on deck during their off-hours or finding a secret spot for a nap, they now took their leisure in the crowded forecastle, where the seas could still pursue them if a hatch was not properly secured. But when the hatches were sealed tight the air grew foul and they sat, soaked to the skin, making muted conversation since a man from another watch was always nearby, wanting to sleep.

Bathing became infrequent since it could only be done on the upper deck, now coated in ice. Patrols were assigned to club the ice away and sand was scattered, so that they might walk about without slipping and breaking their backs.

The rigging being frozen, their mittens were useless so they went aloft with bare hands gripping icy rope. With no proper means of drying their clothes they wore whichever garment was least wet. The occasional snow flurry was a relief, since it didn't soak them as thoroughly as the rain, which fell in sheets from the sullen skies, sweeping across the decks.

The night watch was doubled, with constant vigilance required to keep from encountering any of the icebergs sometimes erroneously hailed as an island, sometimes, improbably, as a sail. There were several close calls.

The storms of course, cared not for the doings of mere mortals, and they lined up one behind another to take a crack at the UnderGod, to toss it about as if there were no men on board at all, no families watching anxiously in the living rooms of far-off North America.

The gales came steadily from the west, sometimes bringing rain, sometimes hail or snow. Occasionally they shifted to a more southerly origin, and because Braga had deliberately taken them far to the south before making the westward turn, they could then let go some sail and the ship would tack its way forward in miserable, barely measurable increments.

Roland lay in his outdoor jail, drenched, writhing, drawing in breath in painful gasps. The maddening restriction of the strait jacket caused his field of vision to contract and darken around the edges. They'd intentionally placed him so he was looking directly up at the flag of the UnderGod and his eyes began playing tricks: he saw armies of crosses advancing on him and in one especially vivid hallucination he watched as the expression of innocence on the face of the Lamb of God turned knowing and despotic.

With Roland the center of attention, scant notice was paid to the small groups congregating around Walter Pickett or to the earnest tones in which Walter spoke of simple justice, and punishment cruel beyond belief, and the need for men to take action if they were still to call themselves men.

There came several days unvarying in their particulars—leaden sky, churning sea, spray washing up over the sides to mix with the unending rain. The sun reduced to memory, the cold a thing to be grappled with.

Luther stood under the shelter of the helm's housing in conversation with Chip Ribbons. A delegation approached.

In their lead was Lieberman, the grocer who'd been taken hostage as part of the practice pirate attack. Lieberman was a man with an uncomplaining face, a long-enduring face, a man who even in his broadest smiles seemed to be suffering from some inner affliction.

Lieberman believed in the basic goodness of men but also in the need for tough action when times called for it. He was actually not a grocer but the owner of a high-end import store specializing in Norwegian delicacies—rare sardines and free-range quislings valued for the gamy, bipartisan flavor of their meat.

Lieberman stood at the front of his little company, smiling his agreeable smile, shifting his weight to withstand the wind's gusts and the rolls of the ship, clapping his hands together not so much to force Luther to acknowledge his presence as in a cheerfully old-fashioned attempt to keep warm.

Luther had caught sight of him a ways off but kept his back turned, making a show of quizzing Chip Ribbons on a technical point of navigation, eventually presenting a puzzled face to the clapping little man, granting permission with a gesture for him to approach.

Captain sir, respectfully, I have been appointed to ask whether we can turn around, Lieberman began, with admirable frankness. Sail the other way, he went on—talking into Luther's stern-faced silence—still accomplishing the UnderGod's mission, Lieberman was at pains to emphasize—but the other way, round Africa, the Cape of Good Hope instead of the impassable Cape Horn.

"Appointed?" Luther inquired, with a forward lean.

"Yes captain, by a group of the men who happened to be talking one day. A rainy day like we've been having, you know how it is, you've told every story about yourself you can possibly think of and word games have lost their appeal and so you're left to going on about the voyage and of course we all want to see it succeed and thought we'd make this suggestion. For your consideration."

"Talking?" said Luther.

"About things, our situation, how hard we're working to achieve a common goal—I'm confident we have a point of agreement there—what I like to call in civilian life an intersection of concordance as a basis for mutual decision making. And it's simply, merely, a request or trial balloon as to how best to meet that common goal in which we all share."

"This isn't, as you say, civilian life. Is it?"

"Gosh no. This is much different. Much more important. So much more at stake in terms of setting a standard for the rest of mankind to follow and remaining true to the divine guidance we're receiving, and, and, all the *good* we know this voyage can accomplish. Which was why our suggestion, really more of a hint, or even a clue, like in a scavenger hunt—"

"And our enemies are real enough, are they not?" said Luther.

"They mean business. I think I know that better than most."

"Would your little group like to run the ship?"

"No sir. No sir," answered Lieberman, giving his head an almost violent back-and-forth movement (and in fact straining a neck muscle in the process).

Luther said, "There's a word for a situation where a group wants to seize a ship from its captain. Starts with an M."

"Indeed!" agreed Lieberman. "I would leap at the chance to apply that label in such a situation, were it to manifest itself. Gladly and without thinking and expecting nothing in return."

"Then let's hear no more on this subject."

"Are you sure, sir, you won't—"

"Sssh!"

Lieberman lowered his voice and drew closer. "Sir, I think you should know, I've taken a sort of informal poll of the men, and your popularity has really fallen off. It's in the single digits."

Luther said, "You think I care a whit for popularity contests? My focus is on the distant horizon. That's where history will make its judgment. Your polls, some day, will come to seem pretty foolish things."

"Is that your final word?"

"Yes. Now leave me alone. Scoot!"

Lieberman turned away, his smile almost as agreeable as before, shrugging at his fellow delegates still hovering in the pelting rain, as if to say I have done my duty. He moved with them in retreat to the decks below—they remonstrating with frustrated gestures; he, explaining in terms of the demands of leadership in a dangerous world and the exigencies of the moment, giving his neck an occasional rub.

"O ye of little faith, eh Chipper?" Luther remarked, once the delegation had gone.

A cry of "Ice on the lee bow!" Hard up the helm!" came from the forward lookout. They peered ahead to spot the floating whiteness. Chip focused his concentration on the wheel. They stayed clear of it.

The temperature took a dip, the rain turning to hail, then snow.

Rob Dawg came aft and saluted, creating a little flurry of white shakings.

"Sir, the prisoner....has been freed," said Rob.

"You mean he's escaped?"

"Not exactly sir. He was let loose, freed. By Braga. Braga cut him loose."

"What about the guard?"

"He tried to stop him. But Braga said Roland was going to die if someone didn't do something.

Luther's features softened. He said, "Roland wasn't looking too good, was he? We probably should have brought him in before this. Braga has saved us the trouble. We made our point. And I know Roland. He can take a hit. Everything rolls off him. He'll be all right. Everything will be all right."

The days passed in little-varying struggle. When a fair wind blew they tried to run before it but the ship tossed in the rough waters and soon the dark clouds would launch at them again, from the west, always the west, and the sail would be hauled in and they'd be reduced to edging forward as before.

There came at last an afternoon when the wind came round fair and the clouds were lanced by a lone ray that held their attention as if it were a miracle, a crying icon, a leaf in the mouth of Noah's dove. Then in a rush the light flooded through in thick beams that found the black-tipped wings of wheeling gannets and turned the sea an indigo blue and it didn't matter whether the light's source was the God of Abraham, a nameless explosion from long ago, or the sparks from the wheels of Apollo's chariot. It was merciful. They had come round the Cape. In a few short hours, they had squared the yards and stood to the north.

The skies now unfolding before them were a revelation. White-grey clouds rising from the horizon, enormous, billowing outward, upward, outlined in shades of pink and coral. In the gaps created by their splendid shifting, glimpses of the true cerulean heavens emerged and then were hidden again.

In the surrounding seas flying fish leapt and spun and fell back into the water, their place soon taken by another with new antics to display. The crew was all on deck. They had feared the Cape. It had seemed certain they would encounter some great defeat in rounding it. That shared experience, coupled with the physical hardship and followed now by the uplift of breaking through to the safety of the Pacific, bound them together more tightly than ever. They were content to stand talking, looking out at the wide expanse of the ocean. Braga set a course for the Torres Straits that separate New Guinea from the north of Australia.

VII

WALTER PAID A VISIT TO the darkened corner of the berth deck being used as a sick bay. No door delineated it, only a decomposing set of curtains that could be drawn in an attempt to keep out noise, or keep in heat. Beds were set in rows and cabinets with glass windows lined the walls, along with shelves overflowing with bottles of medication.

Walter said in a quiet voice that he wanted to visit with Roland. The attendant said in a quieter voice that Roland was sleeping and shouldn't be disturbed.

"I'd lak to, if it's all right, jes' set by him a spell. Sort of pay muh respects."

The attendant allowed it; given Roland's condition, he knew there might not be many more chances for such visits. With great caution Walter placed a chair beside Roland's sleeping figure. He spoke in a whisper low enough that the attendant might think he was praying.

"Wanted to come round an' let yew know I feel badly 'bout yer situation an' partly responsible, too. See, I bin tryin' to provoke Luther into some reactionary behavior, thinkin' he'd do somethin' so repressive the crew would at last reco'nize the reality o' their situation an' rise up an' take command.

"That wuz muh intention. Now it seems lak Luther, fer interpersonal reasons I hadn't allowed fer, has focused his repressive backlash on yew personally. An' fer that I truly am sorry. I thought you two wuz friends.

"It's kinda hard fer me to reco'nize whar muh own self-interest left off and muh desire fer social justice begun. I confess to havin' a healthy ambition fer fame an' fortune. Perhaps too healthy. Yew pro'lly saw that afore I did. I jes' hope it's somethin' yew kin fergive, once yew pull outta this slump yer in. An' I know yew will. We's all countin' on it. Thass' all fer now. I'll be by agin."

In the calmness following the Cape the Opticon Network aired a series of interviews with the families of the UnderGod crew, with an emphasis on wives and mothers.

Blaze Dorsey said how proud she was of Luther that he had stayed the course, and had risen to the challenge of great events by revealing Churchillian depths no one knew existed.

Reenie Rutherford, interrupted in the act of canning blackberries, apologized for being "smack out o' stuff" to offer her interviewers. She was asked about her husband's performance so far.

"Firstly, we ain't never had a proper weddin' so we's not married. Common-law nothin.' So I'd 'preciate yew not dignifyin' his delusions. Second, I don't know whut to say 'bout his performance other than wherever he is, he gen'rally stirs things up. So it appears he's jes bein' hisself an' how high am I supposed to rate that? I'd like to git a ratin' fer my performance but don't nobody seem interested, least of all the man always braggin' on how he's muh husband."

Also aired were snippets from the surreptitiously-filmed lunch between Roland and Blaze, described in voiceover as a date. An indignant Blaze denied any relationship with Roland Orr other than friendship.

As for Roland, the few references he'd provided on his Voyage of the UnderGod application proved impossible to locate. So no one spoke about him except a doctor expressing concern over the possibility of pneumonia.

The UnderGod had now entered the lower regions of the fabled South Pacific. The men resumed their habit of congregating on deck after the evening meal to look out at the sea.

One evening a quiet conversation grew quieter still, then died out altogether.

"Let's have a story," came a suggestion.

"Yes, a story."

"One we haven't heard yet."

"If there are any."

"A good one."

"The best one."

"A contest!"

"A contest for the best story!"

They were of one mind. The evening would drift by so much more agreeably. Who would be the contestants?

"Count me in," said the loquacious Braga.

However, his entry proved an impediment to the whole idea. Braga's prowess as a storyteller was intimidating, his knowledge of sea lore formidable, his repertoire of harrowing tales of survival, exhaustive. Who would take the field against him?

They prompted Walter but he quietly declined, saying, "Kain't spin no yarns jes' now."

"What about you, Lieberman?"

"If that's what the group wants," said Lieberman.

"No! Not Lieberman."

"His stories suck."

"Not much of a contest if only one person enters."

"Very well," said Max Winter, "I'm not much for fancy talk. There's really only one story I know well enough to try to tell. But I know it by heart and believe in it with all my heart. It hasn't been heard yet on this voyage and it should be, because it's the greatest story ever told."

"Ha!" said Braga, grateful for a competitor, even one such as Max. "You're going to recite the New Testament?"

"Not exactly," said Max. "The story begins before that. When the tribes of Israel, God's chosen people, have spent hundreds of years in captivity scattered among the great empires of the Assyrians and Babylonians and Persians.

"They feel abandoned by their God Jehovah, who in former times has led them to mighty victories over their enemies. They don't understand why he has deserted them, since they have not been disloyal. They call out to Him.

"'Wake, Lord! they say. Why do you sleep? Why turn your face away? Arise! Command the sea, as you did when you drowned Pharaoh's armies!'

"Hundreds of years go by, yet still the Lord remains hidden. Now Israel is oppressed by the hated Romans. A young woman, a Jew and a virgin, is engaged to be married. She receives a visit from an angel who says, 'Hail, favored one! The Lord is with you.' She is afraid. She knows not what the angel means. Shortly after, she gives birth to a son in a manger because there is no room at the inn.

"We know nothing of his childhood. At the age of twelve his family journeys to Jerusalem to attend the feast of the Passover as part of a large group. As they depart for home, he is inadvertently left behind.

Frantic—as you can imagine—his parents return for him. They find him in the temple, both listening to the teachers and questioning them in his turn. A mere boy! His parents say, 'Son, why have you treated us this way?' He answers, 'Did you not know I had to be in my Father's house?'

"In each encounter we read of, he displays this curious expectation that people should know who He is and why He has come.

"Once, as he preaches in a synagogue, a man comes to him, possessed by a demon. The demon calls out, 'I know who you are! The Holy One of God! Have you come to destroy us?'

"You see, the demons know him but men do not. Who are you? men keep asking. He tells them but always in coded language. And always, he seems surprised at their lack of understanding.

"He wanders, preaching parables they struggle to grasp, making miracles for a lucky few, biding his time. The poor and meek should count themselves blessed, he says. They will be rewarded not in this world but the next.

"This is His answer to the longed-for return of God's intervention on the side of Israel. Overthrowing the Romans is something he no longer cares to do. He's beyond all that.

"He hints that the miracles he performs are mere tokens of the greater gift He is soon to give. Love each other, He says. Not just with neighborly affection but with the kind of love He will soon display. Love those you haven't met. Love those who strike your face. Turn your cheek that they may strike you again.

"He is captured, questioned. He responds with his usual evasions and unbelievable assertions. They mock Him, spit on Him, crown Him in thorns. His most faithful disciple denies Him.

"He is nailed to a cross. His death is intentional, a kind of suicide. They go to find his body and when they roll the stone away He is not there. This is the fulfillment.

"Do stories have meanings? This one does. Suffering here in this wretched life no longer matters. It is but a thing in passing. We will each of us dwell with God in eternity, find life everlasting if we only believe on Christ Jesus."

There was silence when Max stopped speaking. Such a flood of eloquence from this timid old soul. Who could have predicted it? They felt the ship's motion, a breeze stir then die away. Their eyes fell on Braga. Could he top such a tale?

"It seems Max has me at an advantage," said Braga, heavy-lidded eyes obscured in the gathering dusk, "since the greatest stories always concern the gods. I am familiar only with the stories of men and their explorations of this watery world. It does so happen that the greatest explorers were my own people, the Portuguese.

"The story I will tell concerns Manuel de Sousa Sepulveda and his wife Dona Leonor. And the passengers and crew of the galleon Sao Joao, which left India in 1552 bound for Portugal, carrying pepper and slaves and cloth. It is said that since the discovery of India, no ship had ever left carrying such riches. Manuel de Sousa was its captain.

"It took more than two months for the Sao Joao to reach the coast of southern Africa. Here they encountered storms which tore the sails from their masts and damaged the ship's helm. They floated for weeks at the sea's mercy, hoisting sails fashioned from the woven cloth they had intended to sell at a profit to their countrymen, still thousands of miles away.

"A night came when the winds were so strong the galleon was literally blown apart. Some made it ashore on the ship's boats, others by floating on boxes or the hull's wooden remnants. Many drowned.

"The survivors huddled together on a beach in what is today called Mozambique. They rested a few days, then began a trek northward up the coast in hope of finding a friendly port town.

"One who survived remembered the order in which they marched: in the front a banner and crucifix. Next, Manuel de Sousa with his children. Then his wife, Dona Leonor, in a litter carried by slaves, followed by all the others.

"They proceeded for a month, eating rice salvaged from the wreckage of the ship, and fruit from the trees. They saw leopards and lions, and the leopards and lions saw them.

"One by one the old and weak were left behind. De Sousa's young son was one of the first to be abandoned, although de Sousa was unaware at the time. That night when he learned his son was back somewhere in the jungle, he nearly went mad. He offered five hundred *crusadoes* to any man who would go and get his son. No one accepted; they were too fearful of the big cats and the serpents they had seen on the trail that day.

"They traveled this way for nearly three months, each day bringing new agony. They paid one another to fetch fresh water, the price going up as the journey continued, the value of a *crusadoe* lessening in comparison with the need to go on living. They survived on shell fish thrown up by the sea.

"Manuel de Sousa began to behave erratically. He complained of pain in his head and they bound it with cloth. By now his wife Dona Leonor was no longer being carried on a litter. A delicate noblewoman, she kept up with the rest of them along the rough trails.

"They came upon a native tribe ruled by an evil chief. The chief offered them food and shelter. But he said the Portuguese had to split themselves into smaller groups since a single village could not provide for so many. The chief also required them to give up their muskets because, he said, his people were afraid of muskets and would provide no help if they were in fear.

"De Sousa had grown weary. He did as the king asked. At once when the muskets were given over, the tribe set upon the Portuguese, stripping them of their clothing and jewels and money, leaving them naked and bereft of possessions, as man first was when God created him.

"When Dona Leonor was left without clothes she covered herself with her hair, which was very long, and she dug a hole in the sand, for they were on the banks of a great river. She buried herself to the waist so she would not be ashamed in her nakedness. She told those who remained to continue on, leaving her and the captain and their small children in their misery to die.

"Dona Leonor never moved again from the hole she had dug. Her husband was forced to leave her to go into the jungle to gather fruit to feed her. He did this twice. The second time he returned, she had died. With his own hands, he dug a grave and laid her down. Then he walked into the jungle and was never seen again. That is the end of the story."

There was quiet too, when Braga had finished. What terrible sadness life can bring. Tragedy awaits us all. The men realized they had now to make their choice, and a discussion ensued. But these were simple sailors, lacking an idea of how such a judgment should be made.

"The storytellers must defend their stories," they said. "Make your case. Explain why your tale is greater."

Max went first.

"The life of Jesus brings us redemption, hope, salvation. It encompasses all of history, all of eternity, all of the battle of good versus evil. Nothing can approach it."

Braga replied, "Jesus was God. You can say all you want about suicide and sacrifice, but in the end, right now in fact, Jesus is the omnipotent ruler of Paradise.

"Consider, on the other hand, Dona Leonor. She watches her children die, her husband lose his mind. She trudges on without complaint and in her final hours she refuses to use her noble status to demand special treatment. She dies under the most adverse circumstances imaginable, as a modest woman, her dignity intact."

Max said, "But your story offers no hope. Only sadness."

Braga said, "With death there is finality. The story comes to an end. Then another can begin. This is the ultimate source of hope. But now I'm afraid it is time for these men to assume their duties."

Braga was right, for as he spoke the ship's bells were rung to signal the midnight watch. The men went to their posts without having rendered a judgment.

* * * * *

Concerned over the damage the Cape may have inflicted on the ship, Braga appointed a committee to undertake a comprehensive assessment. On completion, he requested a meeting with Luther, who first put him off to Max, then agreed to meet but rescheduled several times. Braga persisted, eventually securing an invitation to Luther's cabin.

He entered as Luther stood before his mirror, examining himself. Braga noticed Luther's lips were cracked and swollen; he touched his own and realized he was just as bad off. Braga seated himself, taking the opportunity to study the forty-eight inch video monitor used in communicating with Evor Lark.

Braga said, "How often do you talk to them back in the States?"

"Not that often," said Luther, squeezing the folds on his face. "They've turned into such nags. Maybe tomorrow I'll turn it on."

Luther threw himself into his leather chair with a satisfied sigh, long legs stretched before him, arms folded behind his neck.

"So we've made it through after all," he said. "The doubters were wrong. Turn back! What nonsense. Now nothing can stop us. We'll be heroes, eh Antonio? You know, there could be a book deal in it for you."

Braga said, "Luther, I'll get right to the point. I've made a complete inventory. The general condition of the ship is alarming. There are bugs—termites and other insects—running all over the storage holds. They've ruined most of the remaining provisions. We opened the flour barrels and saw weevils and roaches. It would turn your stomach. And there is mold too, from the moisture. Most of the meat is thoroughly infested as well. As for the ship itself—"

Red-faced, Luther cut him off: "Who sent you here? Is this a joke? Why do this to me? Why do you lie?"

"We can see for ourselves if you'd like," said Braga. "The food is not the worst of it. It appears the timbers of the ship are being eaten away by worms even now as we speak."

"The ship!" said Luther. "The ship is newly rebuilt by patriotic naval retirees! It can't be rotten."

"The UnderGod has a double hull," said Braga patiently. "The outer planking is oak, which is a hard wood. But for the inner hull it seems they used a cheaper pine, which is not uncommon, but it's softer and easier for the worms to burrow through, which they seem to have been doing ever since we lingered so long in the tropical latitudes."

Luther said, "It's not possible."

"Like I said, you can see for yourself. Don't look so sad. We were fortunate to make it around the Cape in this old tub. We've done well."

"Old tub!" said Luther. "Now you've gone too far. Admit it. You hate the UnderGod. You have from the beginning. Max told me about the other night and your little story, so tragic and sad. You want failure, you embrace failure."

Braga said, "I'm a sailor. I'm incapable of hating any ship, especially one as elegant as this. Sometimes when I glance up at night and I see these white sails—a pyramid of marble, I think one of your authors describes them—it is moving, unlike anything I've experienced before.

"Still, these heavy guns make it unstable when the seas get rough. I thought we would be swamped more than once. It is true I will not sail on the UnderGod any longer than I have to, now that I know what I know. I'm telling you this for the safety of the crew."

"Then just so we know each other's position," said Luther. "I won't be removed from this ship unless by force. Do we understand each other?"

"Perfectly," said Braga.

"Then let us go and make our visit," said Luther. "As you suggest."

Braga showed Luther the damaged areas, opening up barrels so Luther could see the rotten contents for himself. The steward explained that in his opinion, the infestation of the food had begun when several casks of UnderGrog burst in the heat as the ship languished in the doldrums.

Luther and Braga went up on deck. The sky was spotted with fleecy clouds playing idly with the rays of the setting sun.

Luther said, "What is it you're recommending?"

Braga said, "That we put in on the nearest island so we can make a thorough inspection of the hull, to see if we can continue. At the same time, they could bring us more supplies."

"If we do as you say then we've failed. It would violate the conditions of a successful Voyage—no help from outside sources."

Braga said, "There are lives at stake here."

"Other things too," said Luther. "Even you came to me—don't deny it—when the storms were raging. You made your whispers about turning around. But I kept faith. I believed. And now we're here."

"We can't go on Luther," said Braga. "It will be better for everyone, the sooner you admit that."

Luther didn't answer, but went below and shut himself inside his cabin.

The news of the possibly rotten timber and shortage of provisions raced through the ship and without official confirmation or denial, became distorted, to the point where some of the faint-hearted were for lowering the boats right away, lest the ship sink beneath them all as they slept.

* * * * * *

New York City: in the midst of the mid-morning Manhattan hustle, reporters arriving at the Blomberg Building lobby were directed up a short flight of carpeted stairs to the newly nautically-themed media room. There they found a buffet breakfast laid out featuring shrimp-and-scallop omelets, bowls of whale-shaped wheaties, yogurt in the shape of an ice berg and, alongside the usual coffee and tea, pitchers of UnderGrog.

After chatting informally with select reporters, Evor Lark made his way to a microphone:

"Good morning everyone. Thanks for coming down on such short notice. My goodness, looks like we're all a little thirsty this morning. I'll take your questions now."

Q: "This UnderGrog has quite a kick. Yet I understand you're trying to get it into vending machines in high schools and middle schools?"

Lark: "Let's be fair. The Precepts Corporation is donating an entire UnderGod curriculum to our most needy schools, of which UnderGrog is merely one component. Research has shown UnderGrog calms the hyperactive student and peps up the dullards. Making it available at affordable prices improves test scores and helps students connect with their heritage."

Q: "Evor, there's been a flogging, a person is critically ill, there are major questions about the condition of the ship and its provisions, and there's even speculation some of the crew are developing scurvy. When are you going to pull the plug on this loser?"

Lark: "Wow. That's a whole grab bag of false assumptions and misleading accusations. I only have time to address a few. First, a captain has discretion on whether to apply corporal punishment. This is well-established in the law of the sea and while some may want to second-guess a commander in the field, I say let the professionals do their job.

"Second, doctors and congressmen are monitoring the crew's health by videotape and we'll take appropriate measures if anyone is deemed in jeopardy. And I'm sorry, but I must object strongly to your assessment that the UnderGod is in any sense a 'loser.' This is a good voyage. A successful voyage. Well on its way to accomplishing its mission, creating value for its sponsors and bringing credit to the nation."

Q: "Evor, is the crew being held against their will? I mean, if you watch the live feeds over the net, there's a lot of dissatisfaction. Will they be given an opportunity to get off the ship?"

Lark: "This is a volunteer voyage. No one's compelled. They knew what they signed up for and they know, much better than we—surrounded here by our comforts and enjoying our freedoms—they know what's at stake out there. Sure there's grumbling but they're all on board. So to speak."

Q: "But will they be given a chance to leave the ship?"

Lark: "We may look into that. The logistics would be difficult. Who haven't we heard from? Jeff?"

Q: "Can I just say I admire your patience in the face of the constant carping and criticism that can be so mission-destructive? And FYI, we're out of UnderGrog."

Lark: "Thanks for the heads up and your comment's a thoughtful one. I agree that second-guessing is not a policy. The Precepts Corporation looks forward to a day when the balance between freedom of the press and unity of national purpose can be restored to the Founders' original intent."

Q: "What about reports that the UnderGod is a cover for the search for weapons of piratical destruction? And that they've found nothing?"

Lark: "I can't and won't comment on a report I haven't seen. I'll just say that the crew of the UnderGod—especially its captain—are vigilant and on the lookout as they go about accomplishing the mission of their daily lives."

Q: "Was that a yes?"

Lark: "It was what it was. Listen, I've got an appointment for a deep-tissue massage so I'm going to have to cut this short. You're welcome to stay as long as you'd like. I'm told we're going to roll out some fabulous squid quiche in a minute. Enjoy."

Later, in the back seat of the Precepts Corporation Eradicator, Evor breathes deeply, relaxed but purposeful after some much needed body-work. He fiddles with his cell, trying once again to complete his call. At last Luther picks up.

"Luther, Luther. Long time no talk to."

"I know. It was rough out here for a while. I wanted to focus on the job at hand."

"I understand. But it's really helpful if we can keep in touch a little more. This morning I took some pretty tough questions on your behalf. I backed you up a hundred and ten percent but I've got to level with you, things don't look so good."

"What? Why? We made it around the Cape! That was the hard part. How are the ratings?"

"So-so in the US," said Evor. "The Cape was dramatic and all, but the whole thing was so stormy and depressing, I think some of our core audience switched over to the golf channel for some sunshine."

"Fair weather friends."

"Well, it's a free country. Listen, I don't want to get you excited but I've got some news. We're going to have to get Roland off the ship. We can't have him die on us. I'm arranging for helicopters from a DOD base in southern Argentina. They'll be there in a day or so."

Luther said, "I think that's an excellent idea. Roland is the cause of most of my problems. But you only need one helicopter. Any more might cause trouble. We don't want to start a stampede."

Lark said, "We're getting questions about whether the crew is being held against their will. So we want to send more than one. Then have them come back empty. It'll be a great visual testimony to the loyalty of your men. Think you can manage that?"

"If that's what I have to do, then send half a dozen. A whole fleet. They'll go back empty. I'll bet everything on it."

Evor said, "We are betting everything on it, Luther. It's all coming down to you."

The UnderGod crew sat cross-legged or leaning on the rails, piled against one another in brotherly closeness, a few outliers draped among the terminating shrouds. Brought up from sick bay, Roland was laid out on a stretcher. His shivering gone, he now could sit up a few minutes at a time.

The officers were late, unusual for a general assembly.

When they did arrive they presented a sight more unusual still. They were dressed in peculiar outfits: leg breeches with stockings held in place by garters, and shoes with bulky, brass buckles. Up top, they wore padded doublets with loose fitting linen shirts underneath and a white ruffle surrounding the neck. The whole ensemble topped by a felt hat with a wide brim. Luther's was the color of a plum.

The outfits were historically authentic replicas of those worn by the males of Salem Village in the early days of the republic. Blaze had bought them second-hand from a theatrical troupe funded by the faith-based portion of the NEA budget. Luther had saved them for just the right moment.

"Citizens! Sailors! Loyal crew!" Luther began. "Forgive my attire. I come from the spiritual battlefields."

Hat removed, he made a sweeping bow.

"We're proving them wrong, you and I. We've come round the Cape. Dare I say, mission accomplished? We stand on the cusp of greatness."

He put on reading glasses, patting various pockets in search of something.

"It may not be fashionable to do so but I'm going to read a letter given me just before we sailed, pressed into my startled hands by a grieving mother whose son served in defense of our country as a morale officer in the greater Caspian Sea region. He was excited, extremely excited—ah, here—to learn of the Voyage of the UnderGod, thanks to the miracle of the internet.

"She quotes from an email he sent: 'We are fighting so the Under-God will have the freedom to complete its mission. In the event of my untimely death my last wish is that the UnderGod continue on in the face of all obstacles.' End quote."

Luther removed his glasses.

"His mother adds, in a postscript that greatly saddened me that her son's humvee overturned in a watery canal the next day as he delivered a ping pong table to a nearby base. He was drowned before he had a chance to draw his gun.

"Will his death have been in vain? That question, it would seem, will be answered here on this ship.

"We must remember that the future is not just a door you walk through into a room called tomorrow. Preparations must never cease for the last act of the human drama. And so I state this to our enemies: I've fought you many times over in the bright theater of my imagination. You talk of madness. I tell you I am a servant of One whose purposes are not easily discerned. There's a difference.

"I close now by donning the robes of the prophet as I have already donned, as you can see, the robes of our ancestors. Soon—perhaps before

I have finished speaking for even now I hear a faint droning in the back of my head—the sky will fill with vehicles whose shining blades whirl above us in a dark dance of temptation. Know this: they come not to unify but to divide. And they have been launched from foreign soil."

He raised his voice as he pointed.

"Gaze with me now at the vaulted sky. 'We will hear them before we see them.' Thus do the prophets inform us. Even now, yes! There!"

They turned, staring in wonder at the prophecy's fulfillment: a swarm of black dots—Defense Department helicopters—populating the southern sky. Like spiders emerging from their holes. The crew was transfixed. The UnderGod's lieutenants moved among them, thrusting into their pliant hands miniature replicas of the ship's flag, mounted on little wooden sticks.

Luther's baritone captured their attention away from the frightening flotilla. Waving a tiny flag he said, "I ask only that you carry these near to your heart. Nail them to the mast in case they succeed in shooting down our colors!"

Then the black dots loomed larger, their droning louder; angry, rotor-driven hornets chopping at the air, segmenting it, dissecting it, apportioning it according to the awful physics of their flight.

Arriving in the vicinity of the ship, a single helicopter detached from its swarming brethren and hovered directly overhead. A rope ladder with a stretcher in a sling emerged from its belly and was lowered to the ship's deck.

Skip, Chip, and Rob immediately moved to the ladder's base, facing out at the crew with folded arms and forbidding expressions.

Luther aimed his speaking trumpet upward, intoning, "By whose authority have you come?" His voice was lost in the din of the chopping blades. Braga shouted into Luther's ear that he wanted to get closer to help with the stretcher.

The men remained in place, holding their flags, unable to erase the image of that doomed officer dying in that distant canal. That the helicopters were there to offer them escape did not occur to them. The hovering vehicles appeared only as alien, threatening.

It was now that a chanting began. Growing slowly, with mounting conviction, its hypnotic rhythm filling every corner of the ship:

"Rejectify! Rejectify! Rejectify! Rejectify!"

They held the word before them like a solemn shield.

Luther, pleased, lowered his speaking horn.

"What are you doing there, Braga?" he called over, noticing Braga seemed to be waving up at the helicopter.

"Keeping the sun out of my eyes!" Braga called back.

Luther turned to Roland on his stretcher, raised up on an elbow. Pointing up, Luther mouthed the words: "For you."

Roland waved his free hand back and forth in refusal.

"Go see what the problem is!" Luther shouted to Max, who reported back after a dutiful trot, "He won't go."

"What?" Luther shouted. "What did he say exactly?"

Cupping his hands, Max shouted, "He said he paid for his ticket and wants to see how the show ends!"

Luther resisted the temptation to barrel over and drag Roland across the deck, maybe knock some sense into him as well. He hadn't counted on this. Roland had always seemed keen to leave. So, the helicopters would leave without a single passenger. All the better.

Luther motioned to the pilot, making his own sideways hand movement: deal's off. The pilot was puzzled. It was supposed to be a search-and-snatch operation. Now it looked like there was no one to snatch.

He radioed back to base. Who in turn contacted CENTCOM in Tampa. Who put a call through to the Pentagon. The Secretary of Defense was briefed as he emerged wet from a sauna.

"Great," he said, wrapping a towel around his southern hemisphere. "Just when my pores were all opened up. So it's a floating Waco, eh? Freedom sure is messy. Well, we gave them their chance. Let's pull our boys back."

In under a minute the command, translated into a more standard military jargon, found its way from the dampened corridors of power in Washington to the furthest reaches of the empire in the desolation of the southern continent, then to the lead helicopter still hovering above the white-sailed UnderGod: Operation aborted. Return to base.

Interrupted from a daydream of dog fights mid the black-smoked plumes of desert oil wells burning, the pilot could only think: another wild goose chase. What would the generals think of next? He radioed to the rest of the squadron. They began the wide, turning movement necessary for the long trip home.

Braga saw them begin this banking maneuver. He eyed his still-chanting shipmates. He glanced at Luther, still licking his caked lips in satisfaction.

The thick-roped ladder, bottom rungs gathered in a circle on the deck, reversed itself now with a yank upward, moving in fits and starts and as the last rung went by Braga grabbed for it. He caught on with only a single hand, needing to fend off a lunging Rob Dawg with the other, and began a jerky, swinging ascent.

Seeing Braga's precarious rise, the men of the UnderGod at once sent up the alarm with shouts and sprints aft to the furthest reaches of the ship, waving with increasing energy in a vain attempt to become a part of the helicopter pilot's rapidly advancing field of vision.

Poor Braga, holding on for dear life looked like nothing so much as Mary Poppins *sans* umbrella as the mother bird began her wide-angled turn to catch up with the rest of the mechanical flock. Unnoticed by the daydreaming pilot, his grip made tenuous as a result of the momentary fracas with the ardent Rob Dawg, Braga didn't dare shift his weight to attempt a grab-on with both hands since that might precipitate his fall and so he rode out over the sea, carried away from the UnderGod higher and farther, the agony in his fingers growing greater, changing to numbness; he grew smaller and smaller to those on the ship, becoming a point in the distance, a speck of humanity clinging to life over not the southern-most ocean but close to it, desperately holding on, weakening just at the moment his somewhat secret ascent was to enfold him into the airborne womb of the throbbing vehicle. He fell instead—an awkward, kicking, flailing fall—somehow imagining he could snatch back onto the ladder with his free hand precious nanoseconds after this became a gravitational impossibility and clinging to this belief in the face of all evidence to the contrary he dropped the thousands of feet to the water below.

His neck was broken, it was later concluded, at the point of impact.

VIII

THE BOUNDLESS BLUE SEA. Its surface color results from the absence of the microscopic life forms that lend to coastal waters their aqua-green coloration. In the open sea even the vast clouds of plankton and algae cannot be everywhere at once and so most of the great oceanic regions, depending on the currents' mindless drift, are watery desert. Their emptiness and transparency allow the red and yellow rays of the light spectrum to be absorbed, so that only the cold and terrible blue is reflected back to the human eye.

Beneath the surface a world of uneven contours lies hidden. If the waters were drained away in some great catastrophe—a passing meteor or a loss of faith—here is what would remain: island arcs and dull brown trenches, sea mounts, rocky-terraced cliffs, canyons larger than any on land.

But the waters never drain; they are everlasting. All is swallowed, all absorbed. Half the earth has been dark since the world began, covered in lightless water, fathoms deep, beyond the reach of the proud and grasping sun. No vegetation grows in this abyss. Only rock and clay, mud and sand. It is a world of carnivores where creature preys upon creature.

Here, the undersea mountains lie beyond the reach of the eroding forces of wind and rain. Here, the deep-sea fish, which approach the surface only at night, glow with phosphorescence, eyes grown grotesquely large to compensate for the dim, dim light. Here, driven by mysterious forces, mighty currents stir the waters, more powerful than any that move on land.

Here, floating by in an endless drift to the bottom, the sediments that have accumulated through the millions of years: the husks of plants, the remains of animals, cries of woe from the lips of poets, dust from civilizations that have risen and fallen, washed off the land by river and flood and biblical rain into the sea, the blanketing sea, the sea that surrounds us, the stark, brave, unrefusing sea.

IX

JANGLED AWAKE IN HIS apartment by his jingling cell phone, Evor Lark fumbles for it, stumbles to it, feels through pants pockets in search of it, finally answers it in sleepy greeting.

"Evor? Saul. Hope I didn't wake you."

"Saul! Where are you?"

"Outer Mongolia. Technically China, at least for now but I have my doubts how much longer that'll last. I don't have time for small talk."

"Is this about Braga?"

"No. I know about Braga. That was terrible, tragic."

"He was so full of life."

"Yes. Now he's dead. Even death, I think, we were prepared for. But headlines like these? It's the final straw."

"Headlines like what? I'm not online yet."

Saul said, "CNN.com. Lead story. Above the fold, so to speak. 'Under-God Rotten to the Core'".

"No!"

Saul went on. "I won't bore you with the details but it seems our group of patriotic naval retirees did in fact use sub-standard materials in constructing the UnderGod's inner hull. They admitted it to a reporter. Said they had to cut corners because they doubted they'd ever see the full value of their military pensions. So Braga was right. But that's not the worst of it."

"What could be worse?" exclaimed Evor.

"Apparently the corporation that sold us the UnderGod is owned by a holding company which was part of a shell conglomerate of which one of the larger minority owners are Somali pirates."

"Somali pirates? I didn't realize they had that kind of cash flow. But even if that's true, we didn't buy the UnderGod directly from the Somalis. We were dealing with intermediaries. Surely the American people can see the importance of that distinction."

"It doesn't matter Evor. The feeding frenzy has begun. They'll tear the Voyage apart now. How it was financed, private lives, mine, yours, Luther's. There'll be hearings, independent prosecutors, depositions, leaks. Old grudges being settled. New grudges being born. The jig is up. You've got to pull the plug on it."

"That won't be easy."

"No it won't. And you'll have to do it on your own. I've promised Beth this is the last phone call or email for two weeks. We'll be trekking in the outer steppes of Inner Mongolia. Staying in yurts and drinking horse milk. I'm leaving my laptop and cell phone behind."

"Wow! What an adventure!"

"I've promised Beth a trip like this for years. I'm paying her back for a lifetime of long hours and business trips."

Evor said, "That's so romantic Saul. I'm sure you'll have a great time. Gosh! I should get to work. I've plenty to do over here."

"Get to it son. This is a part of the business you have to learn. It's called cutting your losses."

It was a long conversation between Evor and Luther. Accusations, re-criminations voiced in levels of anger that rose and fell and rose again.

"Cut and run. Cut and run," Luther kept saying. "Call it what you like but that's what it is. Cut and run."

Evor said, "Luther, it's about exercising good judgment, being willing to adapt to changing circumstances."

"Cut and run. Cut and run."

"Luther don't be—"

"What about the men?" said Luther. "Do you think they want to abort? A man like Pickett. Think what this will mean to him."

Evor then said something he later regretted.

"Pickett is a mole, Luther. A spy. He and I have had an understanding the entire Voyage he'll receive a substantial cash payment if he incites a mutiny against you."

Luther was silent. Then he said, "I don't believe you. Pickett's an authentic American. Max vouches for him. He's the last person who would enter into such an agreement."

"Actually he was the first person," said Lark. "After Roland turned me down. Luther, this isn't about who is for or against you. We're not going to broadcast the show any more. That's the reality. The Voyage of the UnderGod is over."

"We'll sail on. In our own reality."

"You'll be just a ship in the ocean. You'll have no audience."

"My God is a watchful God."

"You'll never make it without Braga."

"We will. Max has been studying him, learning from him. And when we complete our mission by sailing into the harbor at Beaufort Island, there'll be plenty of people watching. You'll regret this 'business decision'."

Luther hung up slowly, letting his temper build, ripen. He started with a kicking episode, inflicting much damage on the communications panel, interrupted by a limping trip up to the berth deck to grab a loose oar, followed by even greater wreckage of the expensive, worthless equipment.

Max showed up of course, attuned as always to his leader's mood swings. Closing the door behind him, he watched quietly as Luther systematically damaged their ability to communicate with the world outside the ship. The end result of Luther's destructive outburst was that only a single camera was left functioning, and it was pointed at a pile of rope in a darkened area well below the main deck.

Max and Luther had a talk. Max, it was clear, would be the one to assume Braga's navigational duties. Pickett would be put in chains, as Roland had been before him.

Luther would put them all in chains if he had to.

The Secretary of Defense was letting off steam to his advisers.

"Ever since that fool Dorsey went off to sail the world, every wannabe in this town is out to prove what a hero he is. Senator Kim is lost in the Chilean Andes. Secretary Montvale is hang gliding off Mt. Rushmore and Congressman Rumpus is leading the twenty-four hours of Le Mans—*leading* for God's sake!—and all I do is sit here in Washington and defend the country and do leg lifts."

The phone rang. The Secretary picked up.

"Oh it is, is it? Put him through. Well what is it Lark? I'm a busy man. A destroyer? Certainly not. Helicopters were enough. You know you shouldn't have gotten rid of Braga, he was a real man. Why'd you kill him off? Oh, you don't?"

The Secretary put a hand on the receiver to announce with amused fondness, "Lark says it's a reality show and he doesn't control reality."

He spoke again into the phone.

"Try the EU. They're always in the market for a feel-good operation where they don't get shot at."

Hanging up, the Secretary turned to the room and said in his challenging way, "Who wants to do cartwheels?"

"Sir, there's no time for that. General Wainscot says he needs more troops."

"They all need more troops. You go to war with the troops you have. Listen, work up some kind of statement on Luther Dorsey. Remind everybody this was a voyage of choice. I don't want any further connection to the UnderGod."

One morning Max was hunched over at the helm. He was studying various maps scattered before him and around him and folded into and sticking out of his pockets, and sneaking the occasional peak at navigational notes written in ink on the palms of his hands. He'd taken to wearing a little hat he had fashioned for himself that had tin foil antennae, which he explained were to pick up radio signals from any nearby ships.

A muttering group approached.

"Max, you're no good."

"You're hopeless."

"You don't know where you're going."

"Nonsense," said Max, swiping at his ginger mustache. "Who says this about me?"

"Pretty much everyone."

"But why?"

Chip Ribbons, observing nearby, ran to get Luther.

The men said, "It's below forty degrees. If we were going in the right direction, we'd be in balmy weather."

"The weather's unseasonable, I concede," Max said. "But even the South Pacific has to have winter."

"The snow flurries this morning?"

"Puts the lie to all that talk of global warming."

"Those ice floes we saw last night?"

"Forget about those," Max scoffed. "Those ice floes were in their last throes."

He continued studying his maps and steering, ignoring the men's glares.

Luther appeared, limping badly. "Make way for Luther," Chip called out, but they didn't budge and Luther had to shove his way through, which he didn't seem to mind doing. He turned to face them, standing shoulder to shoulder with Max.

"What's wrong now?" Luther demanded.

"We're heading for the South Pole. That's the wrong direction."

"For crying out loud," said Luther. "Max, are we heading for the South Pole?"

"Certainly not. I have us approaching the island of Tonga."

"That settles it," Luther boomed. "You all want to play navigator now? I'm going to say something to our skipper I want everyone to hear."

He put Max in a friendly head lock, knocking the tin foil hat off into the sea.

Max pointed out, "Luther, I can't steer like this."

Cradling him in the crook of his arm, Luther said, "This is my guy. This is my little sailor. Where he says go, then that's where I go. And that's where we all go. Maxie, you're—"

"Luther, please. You'll embarrass me," said Max.

"It has to be said," said Luther. "People have to know."

"This might not be the right time."

Luther said, "If I'm loyal to a fault then so be it. Maxie, you're doing a heckuva job!"

There was a mumbled response.

"What was that?" said Luther sharply.

"Faith-based navigation!" came the brave cry.

Luther laughed. "'God has made foolish the wisdom of this world.' Max, who said that?"

"God's Son," said Max.

"End of story," said Luther, eyeing them. "Now return to your posts."

The men obeyed, though this time with an exchange of signals and glances, in confirmation of a pre-arranged plan.

They waited until evening, when Luther was dining in his cabin with Max and the three young lieutenants. It seemed ridiculously easy when it happened; they wondered why it had taken so long to summon up the nerve.

They herded together the few remaining Luther loyalists, forcing them below the main deck. Then the hatchway ladders were brought up and armed guards posted. Like that, they had the run of the helm and hatches. With superior numbers and control of the ship's bounty of weaponry, the mutiny was a fait accompli.

They freed Walter from his chains and chose him to be their new leader by unanimous acclaim.

Walter armed himself with a pistol. The men asked him his plan. Walter said they'd head north ("I'm done shiverin'.") The men cheered. A brawny breeze filled the sails and set them scudding atop the waves to warmer climes.

"We'll do away with all this deck scrubbin' too," Walter said.

They cheered again.

What else? What's the plan?

"I'll have to cogitate on it," said Walter. "Might take time." He began a hunched pacing of the deck, his responsibilities already weighing on him.

"Is it true the cameras are wrecked?" they asked. "Does that mean the show's over?"

"They'll allus be filmin'," said Walter. "They got satellites kin see the hairs on top o' yer hairs."

"But the cameras are off."

"How yew know?"

"There's only one that still has a red light on."

"Yew think they kain't rig it so's they filmin' with the red light off? They's watchin' us right now."

From down below a tumult arose. Chanting. On deck they couldn't make out the words.

Still pacing with a furrowed brow, Walter thought out loud. "They'll send a gunboat to prop up their guy. Did it in the Philippines, Nicaragua. Iraq til it became inconvenient. Doin' it now over by that Caspian Sea."

"You sound paranoid."

"That so? See the markin's on them helicopters came t'other day? DOD."

"We're Americans," they said. "We're free. We can leave whenever we want."

"Braga tried to leave," said Walter. "Look whar he ended up."

"That was an accident!"

"So wuz Paul Wellstone's plane crash."

"Who?" they said.

"Zackly," said Walter.

He lowered his voice at the gravity of what he was about to speak. "Might'uv already infiltrated counter-mutineers amongst us."

The men eyed each other. The chanting below continued.

Walter paced and thought, crisscrossing the deck in a worried stride.

"I reckon we'll have to cut back on the food rations," he said. They groaned.

"Don't hardly have none left," he reasoned.

"Luther never cut back the rations," they said.

Nothing was decided. Walter paced and thought.

He lost track of time. They kept coming to him, asking for decisions: about the food, the course to chart, who should stand watch. He needed a plan, needed to think. But he couldn't—not with all that chanting from below—it never ceased.

The wind pushed them north, the ship almost sailing itself; they sped to an unknown destination. The weather grew warm. The men finished off the remaining casks of UnderGrog and rummaged through the store rooms down below, taking what pleased them. Instead of rations being cut, they voted to double them. Walter said nothing.

In the middle of a late afternoon drinking session a drunken, lawless group climbed the mizzenmast, aiming to cut loose the UnderGod's flag and burn it. Others blanched at such a crime: that was going too far. They came to Walter for a resolution. In the midst of the contentious dispute, Walter snapped.

"Lawd o' mercy! I wisht they'd stop that! Whut is it they's goin' on about?"

It was the chanting. It was unceasing and he'd never reconciled himself to it. He had a mutineer hold him by the ankles as he lowered his head down a hatchway to listen, staying frozen in place long enough for his disbelieving ears to make certain of the words:

"USA! USA! USA! USA!"

He sent a man down to tell them to stop. For a while it quieted. Walter's head cleared. He was on the verge of a decision—a brilliant compromise—when the chanting started up again, obliterating his line of thinking. Louder, more defiant than before:

"WE'RE NUMBER ONE! WE'RE NUMBER ONE! WE'RE NUMBER ONE! WE'RE NUMBER ONE!"

"Can't you make them stop?" the men said to Walter.

"Thass whut I'm talkin' bout!" said Walter. "Show o' hands. I'm askin' fer volunteers." As a noise ordinance committee was being organized, a commotion broke out at the hatchway.

All eyes turned.

The chanting had stopped, replaced by another sound they heard faintly at first: steps being climbed, with an alternating thump and bump, as from the dragging of a heavy object. Gradually, Luther came into view.

His linen shirt was ripped at the shoulders so that it was sleeveless; the muscles of his arms sagged with a sad grandeur. His stockings were torn, his head was shaved. His eyes glistened with conviction. In his right hand he held a rope which had been knotted round the battered video-phone monitor. In a hangman's noose.

He gave the monitor a toss, like a circus strongman. It tumbled and skittered across the deck, stopping at Walter's feet.

"That's what we do to traitors," said Luther, advancing.

"Luther, I'm the cap'n now. Cap'n Walter. Yew got to get that through yer head."

"Who are you to command this holy vessel?" said Luther.

"I don't have to be nobody. Mutiny's a equal opportunity perfession."

"I'm the decider," said Luther. "And I decide who runs this ship."

"Yew're the whut?" said Walter.

"The decider!"

"*Dee*-cider?"

"Yeah!"

"Yew mean turn it back into apples?"

"What? No! You know what I mean!"

The terrible blue of the distant horizon was drawing closer...

Luther continued to advance. "You pretended to be loyal. The whole time you plotted against me."

"Easy, Big Luth," said Walter.

Luther faced the spellbound crew. "He's a fraud! Evor Lark told me all about him! You think he's one of you? He really cares? He was a traitor, a paid rebel."

"He's crazy," said Walter. "Yew all kin see that, kain't yew?"

"He'll get a nice cash payout while you all rot in jail."

"I know'd I wuz gonna rebel," Walter explained in a pleading voice. "Know'd it from the beginnin'. Why not get paid fer it?"

"He's a complete phony," said Luther. "Call yourself an art historian. You've never even set foot inside a museum!"

Walter began a slow backpedal. "Museums take time," he said. "Take money. Bus fare, plane tickets, admittin' fees. I had other priorities."

"All your so-called research was looking at pictures in books!"

"The internet too!" protested Walter. "Twenty-seven inch monitor at the liberry I could download on fer as long as a half-hour at a time! Longer if nobody was waitin'!"

"You're completely inauthentic!"

"No! I don't even have dental insurance! Yew don't git more authentic than that!"

The terrible blue of the distant horizon drew nearer...

Luther pursued, a predator with the scent of blood. "What do you believe in Walter? What do you really stand for?"

"I dunno. Single-payer health care?"

"Do you believe in God?"

"In a manner o' speakin'. Metaphorically. As an aid to child rearin', p'rhaps."

"You're pathetic," said Luther.

"Now yew're gittin' personal."

"I believe in a strong and mighty God," said Luther. "That's what I stand for."

Walter's hand edged to the pistol strapped to his side.

Luther said, "Answer one question truthfully, if you still can. Is the UnderGod the greatest ship in the world?"

"How yew definin' greatness?"

"Answer the question," said Luther.

"Just answer the question," Walter's supporters begged him.

"Terms o' size? Cause I know they got cruise liners, they's much bigger'n this ole vessel."

His supporters groaned. "Size doesn't matter!" they called out.

"It's a ship's heart that counts," agreed Luther.

"Ship's heart?" said Walter. "Whar'd that be? Amongst the bilge pumps?"

"Just say it," his supporters pleaded again. "Say we're the greatest ship."

"Kain't say what I don't know to be true," said Walter, even though he knew they would turn on him for this refusal.

Luther loomed before him and said, "Today's sermon I will deliver especially for you. It's from The Book of Setbacks."

Walter drew his pistol.

"Oh, you've got a gun," Luther said, dropping his head as if in submission. Then without warning he charged like a bull. They grappled, he and Walter, locked together like slow dancers at the end of a party, grabbing for each other, rocking, swaying to the rhythm of the ocean waves. No one intervened. Inevitably there was a red flash and a bang and smoke from the powder.

Luther staggered and slumped, red oozing from his side, staining his shirt's white linen. He remained on one knee as Walter backed away in horror.

"Dear God," said Walter. "Whut have I done?"

Skip, Chip and Rob rushed to Luther's side.

Walter said, "Git the medicine kit, somebody. Luther, take it easy. We'll git yew some help."

"Get up Luther!" said Skip.

"You can do it, Luther!" said Chip.

"Show 'em who the Big Dawg is!" said Rob.

"Stay down Luther," said Walter. "Yew need medical attention."

"He wants you to stay down. You've got to show him!"

"How big your heart is!"

"How great this ship is!"

"How strong your God is!"

Luther could hear them, in the back of his head, their urging voices blending with all the others. Slowly he rose.

"Luther, yer gonna make me shoot you agin'."

More terrible....

Luther lunged for Walter and missed, sprawling on the deck. Walter backed away. He couldn't shoot again. Flush against the weather rail, he turned and threw the pistol into the sea. He could see no escape. The crew had drawn in so tightly around the two combatants that there was no room for compromise. It would be a fight to the finish.

Walter leapt onto the rigging, climbing upward. Luther followed, in painful, labored pursuit.

More blue....

Walter reached the highest crow's nest and dove in, determined to make his final stand. Luther arrived, breathing loudly, peering wild-eyed over the side at the wide-eyed Walter. The crew strained their vision to the breathtaking heights as the UnderGod sped forward under bulging sails, heedless of the human drama unfolding in the midst of its proud and historically accurate rigging. No one noticed the breakers toward which they were headed, the recurring lines of foam that result when ocean waves dash against a solid object. It was a surprise to them all when the hull of the food-depleted, bug-infested UnderGod smashed with full force into the crest of a coral reef, one of an ever-dwindling number, perched on a volcanic seamount that had formed in the terribly blue waters long ago in the distant past, before any of the gods had ever been thought of.

* * * * * *

Desmond hated calling Evor so late, but there was no choice.

"Evor? We're getting some really wild footage from the UnderGod."

"What? How? From that one camera?" Evor switched on his night light. "What's it show?"

"We can't tell exactly, but apparently there's been a, a shipwreck I guess. The camera angle is at the level of the water, as if it's a part of the floating wreckage. There's a few lifeboats but not enough to go around. Most of the survivors are treading water. If they manage to get a hand-hold on the edge of a boat, the people already in the boat smash their knuckles and bite their faces."

"Good Lord!"

"Not according to this footage, Evor."

"Have we notified anyone?"

"Yeah, DOD. But they're not responding."

"What does Saul say?" said Evor.

"Can't reach him. Remember? No cell."

"Good grief. I'm in charge then. I'm the man."

"You're the man."

"Say it, Desmond. Say, 'you're da man.'"

"You're da Man, Evor."

"Dang! I'm gonna blow up!"

"Not to be a bubble-burster Evor, but we have to decide whether to air this footage. It's powerful stuff."

"What about Luther? Is he coming across like a leader?"

"Of the Donner Party maybe," said Desmond. "He appears to—we're not sure, but he appears to be wearing an ear ring. He could be bleeding, too."

"Which ear? The gay one?"

"No. The pirate one."

"We can use that. Tough times call for tough leaders."

"And he's shaved his head and he's dressed in some kind of Thanksgiving pajamas. Like from a play when you're in the third grade."

Evor puffed out his cheeks as he considered.

"Geez, if we suppress this we'll be accused of, of—"

"Suppressing it."

"Exactly. So let's be transparent. Put it on the air."

"Roger that."

"And tell them to rev up Saul's jet. I'm going to get out there pronto. Wherever they are."

X

ON THE ISLE OF ST. FOIX, the once-idyllic jewel of the southern seas, dawn begins with a surprise, the supposedly blameless rays of early light tumbling down onto a quiet lagoon, onto a sight to which they are not accustomed: human bodies on the sand, by the score. They are the men of the UnderGod, sleeping, most of them, the sleep of innocence. Made in God's image, they are dreaming unknowable dreams.

Surrounding them the detritus of the mighty ship: oars, mirrors, broken-off pieces of an enormous oaken hull. A spatula stuck with the remains of yesterday's food. An enormous eagle's carved beak and eyes, fierce and uncomprehending.

Roland awakes, squinting at the brightness. He raises up.

Max Winter is lying nearby.

"Luther. Find Luther," Max whispers.

Roland scans the beach. He spots footprints in the sand marked by an intermittent trail of red spatters already drying in the morning warmth. The trail stays close to the surf, then veers up to a village. Yellow dogs eye Roland, panting, snapping with suddenness at the flies tormenting them.

The footprints fade. The ground hardens. The trail of spatters leads to an alley strewn with rubbish, lined by the windowless backs of stucco houses. Small animals, furtive, businesslike, move in and out of the scattered trash.

The alley branches to a road bounded on one side by a rickety fence and the other a line of shacks blaring music, advertising fizzy drinks and DVDs. Standing guard over the makeshift marketplace is a totem pole the size of a coat-rack, carved with the laughing, leering, howling faces of the local gods.

A helicopter snaps out a maniacal rhythm. It passes overhead. Then a drumming sound: from across the grassland comes a parade of sorts, a marching troop of ill-clad soldiers scolded by a commander for failing to achieve a lockstep unity. Roland passes them by.

He sees a team of oxen with rope through their noses resting in the shade. Sitting beside them a stoic minder with a curved stick, and next to him a young boy. "*Big bird, big bird!*" the boy says with an astonished tone. In a dancing, whirling motion with his arms outspread like a pair of rotor blades, he points for Roland to continue on.

The grass thickens, grows tall, turns to trees and a world of chatter and whistle and the monkey's screech. Roland can hear the murmur of moving water. A body up ahead blocks his advance. He sees the remains of a linen shirt, and stockings stained red, and shoes with thick, brass buckles.

Luther's eyes are open but he struggles to speak. Roland kneels to listen. He lays Luther's head on the rotting jungle floor and walks to a stream, using his shirt to carry water back but most of it spills. There are flies on Luther's face. Roland forces them away. They return. He sees that Luther is dead. There is nothing left to do. Roland would never be so sad again.

"Cut!" commands Evor Lark, emerging from behind a nearby mangrove, cameraman in tow. Evor's eyes are dewy.

"Roland, I can't tell you how sorry I am for your loss. I suppose you'd like an explanation. In fact I think you're owed one. We landed here minutes before you arrived. There was nothing we could do to save poor Luther at that point. Then we saw you stumbling along this verdant jungle pathway and we thought well, this is just a moment of human drama too rich, too saturated with authentic human feeling, to pass up. He was a fighter to the end, wasn't he?"

* * * * * *

The wreck of the UnderGod was a complicated affair. The shattered ship was the property of a corporation registered in the Marshall Islands while the ship itself had been licensed in Panama, chartered in Liberia, and its deceased captain was Brazilian, though it had sunk in international waters and the rights to the TV show were held by an American company in the midst of a takeover by an Australian media multinational. Litigation surrounding the Voyage would last for years.

Luther's death was the exception. Once the St. Foix coroner ruled it was from a gunshot wound, an outcry arose within the US for the prosecution of Walter Pickett. But St. Foix was a French protectorate and French authorities swooped in, separating Walter from the other survivors and taking him to Paris, where they resisted all demands for extradition. A sensational trial unfolded, with dual charges of mutiny and murder.

Walter's court-appointed counsel stressed the harsh conditions of sea-going life and laid great emphasis on the so-called *fasciste mentalite* that had prevailed on board the UnderGod, and that would have provoked a mutiny regardless of any pre-arranged financial incentives. As for the murder, it was a clear case of self-defense, they argued. American reporters attending the trial were enraged when an unbelieving public defender pointedly asked one witness whether this 'Jesus' of whom Luther Dorsey had spoken so often had ever appeared on board the ship, or indeed anywhere.

The jury—slim, elderly pensioners and America-hating civil servants who could afford to spend weeks away from their jobs at full pay—acquitted Walter on all charges.

However, freedom isn't free. Walter had nowhere to go. He feared the legal repercussions of returning to the US and was in fact leery of leaving France at all, with 'extra-judicial' operations becoming less and less remarkable in many countries of the world.

So he remained in Paris, a captive celebrity held more or less against his will, longing all the while for the blue-veiled mountains he called home, and the girl he'd left behind. Walter Pickett Fan Clubs sprouted across the whole of France. His wry expression, puzzled and puzzling, appeared on the covers of magazines at markets and news kiosks. His story arc was fresh and appealing: an art-historian-out-of-nowhere who'd stood up to a self-righteous American tyrant. Walter's faltering attempts at speaking the native tongue were dubbed by some as sexy.

He danced the *possoz boogie* at trendy night clubs and introduced a fast-moving two-step move of his own he called the Underjig. The French went mad for it. He strolled the boulevards, sometimes with a fluttery-eyed French actress on each arm. He received a handsome advance for writing his memoir of the Voyage. He emailed back and forth with Reenie. He was hounded by his relatives, who of course wanted a piece of the action now that he was rich and famous.

He took the opportunity to become a frequent, if somewhat combative visitor to Paris' many fine galleries and museums. At the Louvre he deemed the Mona Lisa mannish and not worth the time in line. At the d'Orsay, he dubbed the Impressionists too flowery and blamed them for the Hallmark greeting card company.

Frowning down at an installation piece one day at the opening of an avant-garde gallery on the spruce-lined Rue de Magne, Walter muttered to himself, loudly, as he tended to do when he had the guided-tour ear phones on.

"Ain't it godawful? Janitor might sweep it up after closin' hours, lessen they made a point o' tellin' him not to."

"Zees is a masterpiece," a Museum official said, increasingly irritated with Walter's ill-concealed criticisms. "What ees your objection?"

The surprised Walter removed his ear phones.

"Only I've seen mother robins cough up food fer their young more pleasin' to look at."

"Perhaps it was not zee intention of zee artist to make something so pleezing for you."

"Then he succeeded," said Walter. "In spades. P-U."

"Eh? You want zee artistic experience to be so easy, like zee Layzee boy you Americans sit in all ze day, eating ze fatty snack foods?"

Walter assumed a pugilistic stance.

"Put up yer dukes, monsieur. We Americans is as tough as ever an' I kin prove it."

The disdainful docent only lifted his considerable eyebrows. "I will not, as you say, put up my dukes. I will ask you to leave. Follow zees gendarme eef you pleez."

A stone-faced security guard appeared, slapping black baton on open palm.

"Suitcherself," said Walter, "I been thrown out o' better museums than this." (which was true, following some recent unpleasantness at the *Espace Dali*)

They gave him the bum's rush past the potted plants and ticket takers and out the front entrance and Walter tumbled down steps to the street nearly spilling into a well-coiffed woman with a clipped-on pince-nez, walking her poodle. The poodle bared its teeth.

Two young Frenchmen ably interposed themselves between man and dog. They made peace with the preoccupied woman and, after helping Walter to his feet, the trio crossed over to a public garden filled with beautifully sculpted trees and a playground surrounding a pond where children chased their floating toys. Walter sat on a bench, breathing in the subtle scent of pink carnations. His two companions amused themselves with a *ballon de football*.

A group of youngsters who had witnessed Walter's enforced exit leapt from their teeter-totters and hurried over. They looked American.

"Hey mister! Why did they throw you out?"

"Were you chewing gum?"

"Did you make it pop?"

"Did you get caught stealing?"

Walter said, "Nothin' like that atall, fellers. Jes' a difference o' artistic opinion."

"Then what are you doing here?" asked one.

"If yew must know, I'm waitin' to get hitched."

"Hitched?"

"Blissfully wed," said Walter, still able to wonder, after all he'd been through.

"Huh?"

"Married."

"Married! Where's the bride?"

"She'll be along any minute," said Walter, eyeing his pocket watch. "She sez it's bad luck fer me to see her too soon afore the ceremony."

"Then how come you're dressed like Davy Crockett?"

"This is how folks whar I'm from dress," said Walter, a little annoyed, feeling once more in his pocket for the box with the ring.

"Are you from Appalachia?"

"I am," said Walter, shielding the fading sun with a hand as he surveyed the near horizon. "Surprised little fellers yer age knows 'bout such a fur-off place."

"Are you in a feud with another clan?"

"Do you like NASCAR?"

"Do you eat critters?"

Walter scowled; before replying he glanced once more at the metro entrance where Reenie had said she'd be. One minute she wasn't there and the next she was, in veil and train, several sisters behind her working hard to keep the white gown from dragging on the asphalt pavement as the look-alike group of them struggled across the wide boulevard.

Balancing on her heels and trying to coordinate her movements with her attendants, Reenie smiled at how clumsy she must appear, not graceful as she'd always hoped for. Once safely across the street, she stopped to compose herself behind the muslin veil that fell to her shoulders, but couldn't help smiling again through the *fleur de lis* as her brown eyes found Walter's.

"Mister," said one of Walter's new-found companions. "Did we hurt your feelings? Is that why you're crying?"

"Durn French pollen," said Walter, dabbing at an eye. He made a move toward Reenie but she gave him a stiff arm, saying, "Makeup, Walter. Took us f'rever to git it right."

She looked him up and down. "Yew plannin' on marryin' me dressed lak that?"

"Nothin' wrong with the way I'm dressed," said Walter. "Fact is I'm responsible for a bit o' a buckskin revival here in Paris which as yew should know is the capital o' French fashion."

Reenie managed a smile. "Where we gittin' married?" she asked. "Time to stop bein' so secretive 'bout it."

"Emerald City," said Walter proudly.

"Whut's that?"

"Theme park they jes' opened up. Based on our own Wizard o' Oz."

"Theme park in the middle o' Paris?"

"Shockin', I know. Beauty part is we kin grab a City-o'-Light burger afore the ceremony so there's no growling' stomachs while the preacher's deliverin' his lines. It's right on the way."

Walter tried to get the attention of his two French companions, who had stopped their *football* for a cigarette break and a chat with a mademoiselle.

"Who're they?" said Reenie. "Yer posse?"

"Folks over here call 'em a entourage," said Walter, putting two fingers to his mouth to produce a shrill whistle.

"Fellers!" he called. "Jean-Luc! Pepito! Time to earn yer francs. *Allez, allez!*"

The rest is a happy ending. A man in buckskin—an American original, self-educated, rough around the edges, successful at last, entrepreneurial even. A truly independent thinker disdainful of established authority. He walks with his bride-to-be through Parisian streets; the woman is accepting of her fate, the naturalness of her feelings for this man somewhat puzzling even to her, but she's hopeful in the way of a patient investor who's purchased a distressed property at a fair price. Walter was a bit of a fixer-upper, but the heart makes its own appraisals.

* * * * * *

Roland eventually parlayed his fifteen minutes of UnderGod fame into a resumption of his acting career. It was an environmental picture shot on an island not far from St. Foix; Roland played a Peace Corps volunteer who stumbles across covered-up data showing increasing concentrations of acid in the oceans and accelerating incidents of dumping, too.

The picture ended with an overheated volcano erupting in a violent storm of ash and cinder. The Peace Corps volunteer's girlfriend, Vicky, is in the lava's path but unable to vacate due to the fatal illness she contracted when she was poisoned by a polluter.

Roland's character has to decide whether to leave Vicky to the lava or try against impossible odds to save her. He thought to himself, the first time they rehearsed the scene, that this was a good day, a day to remember. Running in the direction of a smoking volcano to save his beautiful girlfriend. He wasn't sure if the volcano was computer-generated. He wasn't even sure if Vicky was computer-generated. But life requires faith, and faith does not require that its object be real. Only that it be good. And to Roland, it was good.

* * * * * *

The UnderGod's tragic end forced the Department of Defense to back away from its hands-off policy towards the fallen vessel. Military transport flew the dead back to the States. Luther was flown on a plane by himself. His funeral was attended by political and religious dignitaries from many nations.

There was a brittle brightness to the day; a breeze made the flags flap proudly. The sky had never been more blue. Esther Frazier sang a gospel-tinged hymn. Navy flyers flew overhead in wing-dipped salute. Blaze Dorsey was seated on the dais, holding herself proudly erect. Next to her, Max Winter couldn't stop blubbering as Blaze rose to deliver her oration.

She said, "We Americans, who mean only good, have always had enemies. Historians of the future will have to unravel the reasons why. Enemies who have to be confronted militarily as well as spiritually. I think, in a larger sense, in a way they weren't even aware, the brave men of the UnderGod were doing just that: confronting America's enemies with their very spirits.

"I've talked with the families of these men, some still believing a loved one will be found in those far-off waters, clinging to the floating ruins of that great ship. Not one has expressed regret to me at the Voyage or the reasons for which it sailed.

"The Voyage of the UnderGod is the crowning achievement of Luther Dorsey's life. Who else could have overcome those obstacles? Who but he could have captained that ship? His downfall came from being too trusting of those unworthy of trust. Only treachery could sink the UnderGod.

"What kind of man, then, was Luther Dorsey? He fought for what he believed in. He wasn't one for focus groups or tofu salads or electric cars the size of a child's plaything. I wonder sometimes, if there's a place left in this world for a man like him. I hope there is.

"I think of Joshua, at the very beginning of Western civilization, sword in hand. And of David, standing up to the greatest evil of his day. From these giants of the Old Testament an unbroken line can be drawn to Washington, Lincoln, Palin. And now Luther Dorsey.

"We are a great nation. I would urge any who take solace in this man's death, who think it has sapped our will, to think again. By the way he lived and the way he died Luther Dorsey has made the greatest nation in the world even greater."

She stepped away from the podium and watched the pallbearers lift her husband's coffin and lay it in the earth, to be covered with dirt.

* * * * * *

A bottle floating in the open ocean generally travels in circles, moving forward slowly if at all, bobbing up and down as the wave forces pass underneath. Up, down. Up, down. The waves transfer energy; the water doesn't move. The sea would not do that.

Created by wind at distant points in the blue vastness, the smallest waves are first to form, interacting in a clashing confusion. They separate and sort themselves and smoother swells develop and fall in with like-minded waves traveling at a similar speed, setting off on epic journeys for distant shores. There they encounter shallow waters and the wave feels for the first time, the bottom. Friction develops, the wave is slowed. It builds in height, curling over to form a crest. Then a topple and tumble in the shallow surf to meet its foamy end.

This particular day, cold and gray, the waves arrive on shore with stately regularity, like the coming and going of trains. Like thoughts in slow succession.

An elderly man, trousers rolled and moving his arms with purpose, walks in the blurred mist where land and sea are joined.

He happens onto a family: father, mother and young boy in cheerful yellow windbreaker digging castles in the sand with a trusted shovel.

"Out for a walk, Mr. Winter?" says the father.

"Going into town," says Max. "To try that new restaurant. The fancy one with only a single letter for a name."

"I hear it's expensive. Enjoy your meal!"

A beach ball, gaily abandoned, is blown along and taken up by a retreating wave. The sky is full of gulls dropping clams onto rocks, swooping to retrieve them or just beating their wings to stay aloft in the cooling air. Max takes out the radio he carries on these walks, tuning it to a news channel. Traffic, weather. Wars and rumors of wars. Coming toward him, Max sees the four horsemen of the beach patrol.

"Perhaps today!" Max calls out and they wave back.

He arrives at the restaurant, an old white house that's been restored in the neo-conservative style. He asks to be seated on the verandah, with its magnificent ocean outlook.

A waiter smiles down. He says, "Welcome to W. May I tell you about our special tonight? We have a scared rabbit prepared in a prevaricating red sauce. Comes with corn pone and Perle onions in a crème de fantasia."

"Tempting," says the musing Max. "But those rich foods give me acid reflux."

"Of course." The waiter continues in a confiding tone. "If it were me I'd just go for the burger."

"How big is it? I've had a long walk just now and I'm looking for something I can put both hands around."

"Oh, it's a whopper."

"Then it's got my vote."

"Condiments?" the waiter asks.

"Worcestershire. Mayo. Dijon."

"Very good. One WMD burger. And to drink?"

"A red, I would think."

"May I suggest a bottle of our pre-war '02?"

"How would you describe it?" asks Max.

"Bold and liberating. Not afraid to take chances."

"Perfect."

The evening breeze blows in, tenderly. Max toys with his silverware, thinking. The waiter brings the wine. Time goes by in reflection. Nothing compares to the ocean's waves, we hear in them what we want: nature's beauty, its savage power, its beating heart. The bottle is half gone. Max catches the waiter's eye.

"I can't imagine what's gone wrong," the waiter mutters, going away.

Max has a look inside at the main restaurant: the glistening chandeliers, tables impeccably set, napkins folded, gleaming glasses of water. He notices he is the only customer. The wait staff, so numerous earlier in the evening, are now nowhere to be seen. He feels a gnawing in his stomach. He gets up to find the waiter.

He has a look in the men's room, in the back. Even in the kitchen.

He calls out:

"Where are you? Where are you?"

His voice clangs, echoless, off the kettles and pans hanging from the walls and ceiling.

Back out on the porch he sits to continue his wait—a little miffed, let's say it plainly. But he remains in his seat, in patient expectation, like a character in an existential play. He may be there still. Something keeps him seated, a loyalty perhaps to an order placed and not received. Or maybe the ambiance, somehow down-home despite all the sparkle and glitter. Or maybe it's that to get up and leave would betray a lack of faith and then where would Max be? On his own, adrift in a silent universe, a stream of atoms falling through a void.

About the Author

KIRBY SMITH is the author of *O! Hasenfus!: the agony and the ecstasy of the Iran-Contra Affair* and *Creepicus: a Greco-Roman re-enactment of a presidential tragedy.* He lives in Oakland, California.

CPSIA information can be obtained at www.ICGtesting.com
Printed in the USA
LVOW13s0937070714

393186LV00001B/1/P

9 781940 423029